拒绝合唱

——当代世界英文女性小说研究

Writing Against the Grain：

Contemporary English-language Fiction by Women Around the World

张　磊　著

ZHANG Lei

中国财富出版社

图书在版编目（CIP）数据

拒绝合唱：当代世界英文女性小说研究 = Writing Against the Grain：Contemporary English-language Fiction by Women Around the World：英文/张磊著.—北京：中国财富出版社，2015.12

ISBN 978-7-5047-5928-3

Ⅰ.①拒… Ⅱ.①张… Ⅲ.①英语-妇女文学-小说研究-世界-现代-英文 Ⅳ.①I106.4

中国版本图书馆 CIP 数据核字（2015）第 257984 号

策划编辑 张 茜 **责任编辑** 沈兴龙 徐 宁
责任印制 何崇杭 **责任校对** 杨小静 **责任发行** 斯 琴

出版发行 中国财富出版社
社 址 北京市丰台区南四环西路 188 号 5 区 20 楼 **邮政编码** 100070
电 话 010-52227568（发行部） 010-52227588 转 307（总编室）
010-68589540（读者服务部） 010-52227588 转 305（质检部）
网 址 http://www.cfpress.com.cn
经 销 新华书店
印 刷 北京京都六环印刷厂
书 号 ISBN 978-7-5047-5928-3/I·0207
开 本 880mm×1230mm 1/32 **版 次** 2015 年 12 月第 1 版
印 张 4.75 **印 次** 2015 年 12 月第 1 次印刷
字 数 123 千字 **定 价** 25.00 元

Preface

It can now be safely stated that contemporary English-language fiction written by women has indeed breathed a new breeze into the literary world in more than one way. Compared with their literary mothers and grandmothers, contemporary women writers have made obvious breakthroughs in writing space, literary themes, as well as (especially) narrative strategies.

In writing space, contemporary women's fiction in English is no longer strictly limited to that in Britain and the United States. In fact, it has blossomed all around the world, stretching all the way from Ireland to Cyprus, from Jamaica to Samoa, from India to Nigeria.

In literary themes, contemporary women's fiction in English is full of diversity and complexity. Some of them continue to delve into the necessarily intricate relationship between the two sexes, or the equally ambivalent relationship between the mother and the daughter in a new context. Others tend to investigate the various dilemmas of professional women today. Still others interest themselves in the interaction between women and wars, or the interaction between women and national politics. In most of their fiction, all these issues are seldom separate. Instead, they are often interwoven with each other, making the narrative unprecedentedly profound and thought-provoking.

In narrative strategies, contemporary women's fiction in English merits our especial attention. Generally speaking, despite the visible differences in various texts, contemporary women's narrative strategies are invariably characterised by unprecedented audacity and relentlessness, largely subverting "History", or the male-dominated narrative discourse. At the same time, contemporary women also make unending efforts to rewrite their "her-stories", or the unique, alternative discourse that can give eloquent voice to women's long-hidden thoughts and passions. Specifically speaking, these literary strategies mainly concern the empowerment of women through space, body and voice.

First and foremost, contemporary women writers in English have started to radically challenge the taken-for-granted legitimacy of "house" "room" and "home", all signifiers of traditional patriarchy. Instead, they tend to actively explore and expand space for their own living and development. Actually, this question was raised in as early as the early 20th century by Virginia Woolf in her celebrated *A Room of One's Own*. For Woolf, the reason why women writers cannot get wide recognition lies in the fact that they are lacking in a necessary and independent room of their own for living and working, thus largely restricting the full display of their talents and individuality. Today, despite the fact that it is not as severe as before, the problem of lacking a room of one's own still persists in subtle and yet unmistakable ways. Therefore, it is still of great necessity and urgency to find or construct space that truly belongs to women without male intervention. For instance, in her celebrated *Housekeeping*, Marilynne Robinson from the United States eloquently probes the dynamic and mutually shaping relationship between the modern female identity and the idea of home.

The second site for contemporary women writers' self-empowerment is the female body. In not a few novels and short stories, contemporary women writers have strongly questioned the patriarchy's pervasive regulation and control of the female body, and actively claim its agency and independence. In 19th century fiction, the presence of the female body is often deliberately erased or downplayed, as if it merely means something bad: seduction of a male, or damage to ideal femininity and virtues. The only positive function for a female body at that time lies in mere reproduction of offspring. Any transgressive act that goes beyond merely reproductive functions often ends in the severe punishment of women, as is shown in *The Scarlet Letter* and *Adam Bede*. However, in contemporary women's fiction, this all-too-passive treatment of the female body has been much changed. It has become an active and crucial means of (re) shaping a woman's subjectivity and self as well as a radical means of defying the order of patriarchy. For instance, in her all-too-famous *Lilian's Story*, Kate Grenville from Australia manages to espouse a new and radical kind of feminism through nothing but the grotesque, unregulated and ungovernable female body as the symbolic site of female power.

The third departure that contemporary women's writing in English makes from previous fiction lies in the unprecedented prominence of the distinctly female voice. Instead of being silenced by patriarchy and then getting used to voicelessness, not a few heroines in contemporary women's fiction in English tend to express themselves directly and loudly, without fearing or yielding to the patriarchal discourse. No matter if they eventually succeed or fail, their attempt to voice themselves in a daring manner is indeed laudable, showing a markedly different epistemology that is truly contemporary. For instance, in *The Bastard of Istanbul*, the Turkish writer Elif Shafak manages to empower an entrapped, en-caged, and imprisoned Turkish woman with a strong capacity for uttering her voice, which daringly defies various age-old patriarchal ideologies, especially the severely punitive Islamic law of the father.

The last but not the least feature that contemporary women's writing in English bears is the creative employment of a double as the vehicle of personal revelation. For example, in *The Pakistani Bride*, not only does she offer a convincing portrayal of the Pakistani bride herself, famed Pakistani writer Bapsi Sidhwa also aptly introduces an American bride to a Pakistani Major. Despite their non-acquaintance with each other, the American bride indeed bears a great resemblance to the bride from Lahore in their initial shared romantic fantasies of the "exotic" and later "shared suffering" in a hostile men's world. What's more, the American bride's timely outburst is subtly and yet unmistakably instrumental in changing the Major's attitude towards her and eventually all women, including the runaway bride.

Despite the breakthroughs, especially in the skillful employment of new narrative strategies discussed above, contemporary women's fiction in English still has its own limits. First, in spite of their increasing audacity, their feminist agendas are sometimes easily compromised in harsh contexts, and their female voices also lack a certain coherence, sometimes even contradicting themselves. Second, in spite of the global nature of contemporary women's writing in English, not a few women writers' feminist concerns are still quite narrow and self-enclosed, thus unwittingly isolating themselves from others in their common pursuits.

Of course, generally speaking, there is no doubt that contemporary women's fiction in English has indeed made and will continue to make a big difference in today's world in many ways, both directly and indirectly. There is every reason to make their eloquent and inimitable voices heard by both Chinese and international readers in a timely manner.

Contents

Chapter 1 The Dilemmas and Struggles of Female Intellectuals and Artists: Reading Anita Brookner's *Falling Slowly* (Britain)

"Novels like hers are why we read novels." ——*Christian Science Monitor*

"Anita Brookner works a spell on the reader; being under it is both an education and a delight." ——*The Washington Post Book World*

When praises and acclaims like this are offered to someone like Tolstoy or Dickens, readers tend to feel more than at ease. However, when they are lavished on a contemporary female British novelist like Anita Brookner (1928–), most of us may reasonably raise an eyebrow: Why? What is so different about her? Does she really deserve them?

The first interesting thing to say about Ms. Brookner is that she never intends to be a novelist. In fact, prior to the publication of her debut *A Start in Life* in 1981, at the age of 53, she was most reputed to be an influential art historian, especially of the 18th century French painting. In 1967, she became the first woman to hold the Slade Professorship of Fine Art at Cambridge University. She was promoted to Reader at the Courtauld Institute of Art in 1977, where she worked until her retirement in 1988. Such highly professional achievement in art does not necessarily lead to a literary path. According to Brookner herself, she writes novels simply for a change, or to idle away the time. There is no lofty aim inherent in this attempt. This explanation certainly fails to satisfy our expectations of what a writer should have in mind when writing.

Brookner's statement is both apt and insufficient as an explanation for her writing. The aptness lies in the fact that she never consciously intends to write with the deliberate gesture of a writer, which is more akin to a skilled performer. The insufficiency, however, lies in the fact that she consciously or unconsciously hides the tremendous importance of writing novels to herself. Committed to art and unmarried for life, she simply has too many tales of blessings and curses to tell about herself, both as a woman and a female artist in the contemporary urban world. Her sharp eyes trained in art, together with her skillful and precise execution in dealing with words, further make her an ideal (if late) bloomer in fiction writing.

Following the realist traditions of 19th Century masters like Jane Austen and Henry James, though certainly with a refreshing contemporary twist, she manages to vividly portray the often complicated and ambivalent female psyches in addressing such issues as self, love, sexuality, art, life, and their conflicting and irreconcilable demands in urban society in her twenty-four novels (and *At The Hairdressers*, her latest novella in 2011, available as an ebook only)① . First pub-

---

① Brookner's consistent focus on such noticeably woman-centred themes is sometimes criticised as "too narrow" or "too repetitive" . There is no doubt that Brookner is indeed a writer who is obsessed with a subtly feminist (or post feminist, aesthetically feminist) consciousness, endlessly and carefully ploughing her own terrain, and offering moving variations on the theme of "woman" in contemporary society— "different casts, same script" . However, instead of being a limitation, this is exactly where her strength lies. Some critics even believe if Henry James is around now, Brookner is the only one he will truly approve of. Other critics also duly compare her so-called "narrow" narrative focus to that of Jane Austen, believing them to be both great artists of middle-class domesticity and womanhood. Still others argue that how to write is certainly more important than what to write. Brookner's control over her own material is certainly absolute, which more than justifies her writing practice.

lished in 1998, *Falling Slowly* may be less well-known than her 1984 Booker Prize winner *Hotel Du Lac*. However, the typically Brookerian theme of a woman and female artist's many dilemmas, as well as her often failed and still meaningful struggles undoubtedly reaches a new height in this artistically impeccable novel, thus making it an even better choice for new readers of her fiction. Specifically, the dilemmas that plague the Brooknerian heroines in this novel can be summarised as follows.

Oscillation between "Here" and "Elsewhere"

For Brookner, home is both present and absent. Apart from three years in Paris, she has lived in London all her life. However, she has "never been at home, completely."① This is by no means a high achiever's affectation, but profoundly sincere. As the only child of Polish Jews, she understandably keeps a certain distance from those native Londoners. At the same time, her apparent lack of interest in Jewish matters, including its culture, language and customs, equally displaces her as an outsider. In other words, she feels doubly isolated and alienated, with neither to rightfully call "home".

The profound sense of homelessness easily finds its echoes in *Falling Slowly*. From childhood, the Sharpe sisters, respectively named Miriam and Beatrice, fail to find warmth and comfort in their family, which is populated by their patriarchal father, their grudging mother,

① Shusha Guppy, "Interview: The Art of Fiction XCVII: Anita Brookner," *Paris Review*, 109 (1987), 150.

and their largely indifferent grandmother, who often wage cold wars in the presence of the children. They never stop dreaming of a better home other than the one they have—always "on the lookout for signs of a domesticity that was foreign to their own circumstances" (171)[1].

This secret wish for substitution lingers and well intensifies into their adulthood, which seems to promise in more than one way an alternative to their unhomely home, especially after the death of their parents and their gaining financial independence. However, this promise fails to materialise into reality, for "home" remains as, if not more, slippery and largely illusory as before. In the cosmopolitan world which largely resembles the bleak wasteland in T. S. Eliot's poetry, the grownup sisters still feel trapped, imprisoned, en-caged, profoundly lonely and isolated, leading a mere existence characterised by boring routines and suffocating familiarities. In fact, everything "here and now", including the various streets in London, the bus, the taxi, the library, the museum, the sky, and even the rooms of their own, seem to merely make the Sharpe sisters (especially Miriam) sad. Everyone "here and now", including their nosy neighbours and their practical employers, is less than friendly (if not hostile), constantly intervening in their life in various guises, seeking potential control over them. Even the sisters' mutual presence in each other's lives sometimes makes them uncomfortable and profoundly anxious.

If London, or a London flat "here" lacks a certain "transcendence" (3) that is the mark of an ideal home, the Sharpe sisters' at-

---

① Anita Brookner, *Falling Slowly* (New York: Vintage Books, 2000). Subsequent citations to this work are given as parenthetical page references in the text.

tempt to find it "elsewhere" turns out to be futile and disappointing as well. For instance, for Miriam, Paris offers an Edenic refuge to which she can escape and liberate herself. However, this badly needed refuge turns out to be a merely temporary one, equally problematic, equally full of uncertainties and unexpected annoyances. In a highly symbolic scene, Miriam the householder-turned-into-tenant, discovers to her dismay that a less cultivated neighbour even litters before her very door. There is no point in making a row, for her status as an exile and an outsider can hardly win sympathetic responses from others. She can do nothing but go back to London, despite her great unwillingness. Fortunately, back in London, she finally gathers her faltering courage to recognise her true situation and adopt a right attitude towards life: "She had a long winter to survive. It would not be easy. But she saw, for the first time perhaps, that if careful attention were duly paid, it might, it could, be managed." (227)

As can be seen above, neither "here" nor "elsewhere" can offer an easy and convenient space for the Sharpe sisters, especially Miriam, for the apparent geographical heterogeneity conceals a striking homogeneity that ultimately reduces everywhere to being a hostile presence, thus displacing everyone to the status of spiritual orphanage. Only when one comes to terms with this reality (this does not simply mean bowing to it), can one find inner peace and learn to struggle for an individual's development in a brave manner.

Imbalance between Career and Womanhood

Despite her brilliant career as an international authority on painting, Brookner cannot help lamenting over her single-hood and childlessness as her two great failures in life. Compared with those women who manage to strike a proper balance between career and womanhood, she certainly feels greatly inferior.

This sense of failure registers clearly and deeply with both Sharpe sisters. On the surface, they both excel in their careers, whose achievements far exceed those of their peers. Beatrice, the elder sister, is a talented pianist, who is frequently invited to perform classical music before large crowds and is rewarded in both name and financial gains. Miriam, the younger sister, is certainly no less successful than Beatrice despite the non-sociable nature of her work as a literary translator. Without the constraint of office hours or the fear of unhandsome salaries, she can lead a decent and respectable life.

Ironically, neither sister can gain true satisfaction from their careers, not to mention occasional hatreds for them. For Beatrice, her career as a pianist is hardly inspired, and the constant exposure to the judgmental gazes of the audience in playing often causes her untold fear and anxiety, sometimes even bringing her on the brink of insanity. Therefore, apart from being a means of gaining independence, this career is in many ways "a mistake, a misadventure" (181). As if this is not bad enough, Beatrice is later even deprived of her livelihood with the arrival of a new agent. For Miriam, the situation is hardly better. Despite her reliability as a translator, her work is often taken for granted. Besides, her day-to-day regular life of words and paper takes on an increasingly monotonous and mechanical nature, making her restless.

What's worse, this obsessive pursuit of career is made at the cost of their personal life. Compared to other "ordinary" women of domesticity, they are less than happy. In girlhood, they are trained to lead a practically austere and all-too-innocent life, endlessly repressing their sexuality. When they are finally grown up, they are still unequipped with the knowledge of how to properly love and be loved by men. Specifically, they have no idea of how to "seduce" men by dressing properly and making their bodies attractive. Neither do they show sufficient confidence in themselves. Therefore, their ignorance in the art of courtship and the lack of proper men for them to choose from contribute to their unwise choices in finding partners again and again.

For instance, despite her beauty and talent in music, Beatrice attracts only those old and ill-intentioned married men, who treat her as nothing but an occasional plaything. Among them, her ex-agent Max certainly provides one of the most unappetising, most insincere cases for scrutiny. Not only does he easily shrug off his duty to help Beatrice keep the job of an accompanist, he also goes further by abandoning her as a lover as soon as he discovers warning signs of her dying.

Compared to Beatrice, Miriam suffers even more setbacks in love by being deserted by three men. Her marriage to Jonathan Eldon is based not on long-term and steady affection, but on their mere acquaintance and their mere need to marry someone. Therefore, when Jonathan feels tired of her and leaves for Canada, the divorce comes almost naturally. Her very accidental affair with Simon Haggard, the second man in her life, turns out to be a graver mistake. In fact, apart from his looks and manner, he is one of the most morally reprehensible male characters in a Brookner novel. He is married, self-centred, and utterly conscienceless. In fact, he is the very man who coldly cancels Beatrice's contract. The irony is that Miriam gets involved in this fatal affair with him at no other time than when he comes to inform her of this news and then leaves her flat. What is even more ironic, he, the very opposite of everything good and virtuous, is wrongly seen by Miriam as a messiah figure[①]. The following affair with him not only puts Miriam at the risk of moral accusation, but also resembles a perverted and sadist game, with Miriam as its helpless prey, who is constantly cheated, and left aside with his deliberate absence. To the readers' shock, Simon's playfulness with Miriam only makes her more attached to him, endlessly and hopelessly waiting for him to be back, and vigilantly listening for any steps that may be his. The sad thing is, even when Tom Rivers (a meaningful rewriting of John Rivers in *Jane Eyre* in contrast to Rochester), the real rescuer comes into her life, Miriam is still subjected to the control and manoeuvre of the largely absent rogue, Simon (the worst version of a contemporary Rochester), internalising his demands on femininity. Therefore, she declines the love offered by this potential suitor. Later, only when she unexpectedly runs into Simon flirting with her mistress, does she feel the unworthiness of her one-sided attachment to him. However, when it finally dawns upon her that Tom is the man she should cherish, he has left for Jakarta on a plane, which unfortunately crashes into the sea with no survivors on board, thus ending once for all the possibility of her salvation. As if Miriam's fate is not tragic enough, Jonathan, her ex-husband, whose

---

① Cheryl Alexander Malcolm, *Understanding Anita Brookner* (Columbia, South Carolina: University of South Carolina, 2002), 190.

new wife abandons him for another woman [1] comes back to England, and unashamedly asks for her hand again, based as usual on practical grounds. This time, Miriam finally stands her own ground and daringly refutes his shameless demands.

For both Beatrice and Miriam, failing to find ideal partners is only part of the curse imposed on them for the pursuit of their careers. A more fatal blow to them, especially Miriam, is their deprivation of motherhood. In the absence of good men to love and care for them, they are not blessed with children for comfort and happiness, either. When they chance upon other mothers loving their babies, the sense of loss and hopeless longing is acute, with no one to tell about their pains and sufferings, not to mention their profound sense of inferiority for their barrenness, a failure in the Darwinian selection[2].

Fortunately, just as Beatrice rightly predicts before her death, Miriam is still left with the chance to be saved. This chance happens at the most unexpected time and on the most unexpected occasion—during a conversation when Jonathan returns to England with the purpose of getting back to Miriam. When Jonathan dismisses Miriam's affairs with Si-

---

① Factually speaking, Anita Brookner is certainly by no means a lesbian. Neither is lesbianism a much-discussed topic in a typical Brooknerian narrative. To some extent, plotting such a scene is very probably a deliberately "feminist" gesture that comes as a strong counterattack against men's constant and yet often justified betrayal of women.

② Darwin's evolutionary theory that highlights "the survival of the fittest" finds an unsettling echo in Brookner's many female protagonists, including Miriam and the earlier Frances Hinton in *Look at Me*. They tend to be fatally attracted by handsome and yet morally reprehensible men, unduly heightening their importance at the cost of their own humanity. For some critics, this may qualify Brookner as a committed feminist (although Brookner herself never claims to be one), but it does highlight a woman's true dilemma of "to be (a feminist) or not to be (a feminist)".

mon and Tom as mere things in the past, Miriam suddenly realises that they are "both in the past. But still very present" (223). In their absence, Miriam finally understands the gladdening fact that "she had had meaning for both of them" (223). Her onetime devotion is not in vain as she used to believe. Besides, there are "to be no more inequalities: praise and blame were irrelevant" (223). Both of them now assume "hieratical status in her eyes" (223), with her as "their guardian" (223). This epiphany is by no means a self-deceptive way of comforting her failures as a woman. Instead, it shows that Miriam has come to terms with her wrong choices and losses. In a sense, Miriam's claim to be these men's "guardian" can be interpreted as a quite subversive discourse that inverts the traditional roles constructed for men and women, as well as a confident declaration of her spiritual independence as a new woman.

As can be seen above, for women in contemporary society, a worthy career, in spite of its availability, still imposes much harsher demands on them than on men. What's worse, the frequent and sharp conflicts between a woman's pursuit of an ideal career and her equally rightful pursuit of an ideal lover or husband often throws her into utter confusion and chaos. "Both...and" often turns out to be "either/or". Making either choice is bound to bring regret into a woman's life, cutting the "complete" "her" into half. Only when a woman fully realises the importance of her own position as an active subject in sexual politics, namely not merely being loved and owned like the exclusive property of a condescending man, but seeking due love from a man on an equal basis, can her salvation really come.

Tension between Aging and Innocence

For Brookner, aging is an unsolvable problem that constantly preoccupies her mind. She has closely followed the decline and death of her own mother, her only long-term companion in life. She herself has experienced several attacks by illnesses, the latest of which almost claimed her life. This is even shown in her careful evasion of her true age when publishing her first novel, changing fifty-three into forty-three.

Just like Brookner herself, *Falling Slowly* is also populated by middle-aged women and men. For the Sharpe sisters, aging is a problem that they are utterly unprepared for and utterly fearful of. On the one hand, it poses a larger-than-life threat to both their very being and their hard-earned dignity, especially after they witness the death of their own parents after a stroke and the helpless collapse of an unknown old woman after a fit on the street. In fact, although directly caused by a car accident when she insists on crossing the street to buy things for herself, the final death of Beatrice is still partly a consequence of her increasing fragility and worsening illness, due to which she even gloomily predicts her own end in a hospital or a nursing home instead of her own home, just like her mother. On the other hand, it also renders them increasingly unattractive, unwanted, and undesirable in a highly competitive world, especially when compared to younger people. Being subject to the patriarchal gaze is certainly humiliating enough for a woman. However, if she loses the qualification or the potential for being gazed at, she even loses the possibility for being humiliated, which is paradoxically even more humiliating.

Ironically, despite the physical aging of their bodies, the heroines still retain an innocence or even naivety in mentality that does not quite become their age. Instead of getting accustomed to their present reality and learning to be wiser, they still indulge themselves in various girlish dreams and fantasies, largely created or nourished by their undifferentiated reading of romantic fiction full of overly idealised men and women. Between the sisters, Beatrice is certainly the archetypal idealist by constantly reading various "stronger reading matter" (25) about women, no matter "if the subject were well-bred adultery in a rural setting, or a feisty investigation by a female detective living with her cats in San Francisco" (25), and even foolishly following these largely non-exemplary heroines in her own life— "like all romantics she responded more to outward appearance than to a consideration of worth or merit" (189). Compared to her, the self-proclaimed practical and realistic Miriam is no less idealistic, as is shown by her equal swiftness in falling trapped into the hands of physically advantaged men without doubting their potentially problematic morality. In the end, they are practically bound to be utterly disappointed and badly hurt by their lovers, who have no remorse for their betrayals.

Fortunately, Brookner finally manages to resolve this hopeless and bleak tension in an imaginary manner. In a highly symbolic dream, Miriam embarks on a journey to a mystical resort, where she sees several old women "looking concerned and unhappy" (225). Instead of indulging in unhappiness together with these equally traumatised women, she "advanced joyfully towards them, breathing in the brilliant air" (225). If these old women can be seen as Miriam's doubles or other split selves, Miriam in the dream certainly symbolises her bright and potential heroic side that is eager to rescue her other selves. Interestingly, at this moment, Miriam wakes up, but "with a feeling of extreme gratification, as if she had recently returned from a successful journey" (225) . The word "gratification", noticeably modified by "extremely", convincingly shows Miriam's imaginary success in integrating her various selves and becoming whole again.

Be it the oscillation between "here" and "elsewhere", the imbalance between career and womanhood, or the tension between aging and innocence, the Brooknerian heroines in *Falling Slowly* indeed suffer greatly in a hostile enough age and world. Fortunately, instead of becoming helpless and passive victims of these various dilemmas, they eventually manage to find various effective strategies and means for their own salvation and the reshaping of themselves into complete and new women. In this sense, Brookner is indeed a feminist—not one in personal practice, but a convincingly aesthetic one in words full of visions and emotions, which may be more profoundly meaningful and inspiring.

Chapter 2 On the Exploration of an Authentic Female Self through Transgressive Sexuality and Its Limits: Reading Claire Keegan's "Antarctica" (Ireland)

"With *Antarctica*, Claire Keegan presents us with a series of small worlds under glass, that you shake for snow. Wonderfully detailed and vivid, these are stories of complicity and escape. She is quite unafraid."

——Anne Enright, Booker Prize winning author of *The Gathering*

"Keegan transcends well-worn themes of adultery and familial discord, fashioning resonant stories with fairy-tale simplicity."

——*Newsweek*

Reading Claire Keegan (1968–), the prodigiously gifted Irish writer, is by no means an easy and comfortable experience. *Antarctica*, her Rooney Prize winning debut collection of short stories, best displays many of her narrative strengths, not the least one of which is her capacity for disturbing and unsettling readers with various moral ambiguities still inherent in contemporary domesticity, including love, passion, and marriage. In its title story, through the re-working of the seemingly well-worn theme of a wife's quest for other partners other than her husband, Keegan makes a daring foray into the potential for seeking an authentic, independent female self through the agency of transgressive sexuality, as well as its limits and dangers in a still largely patriarchal society.

Initial Subversion of the Conventional Plot in Complicity with the Patriarchal Ideology

From the very start, Keegan's unnamed female protagonist poses a serious, unashamed, and utterly direct challenge to readers' moral expectations: as a happily married woman, she is still going to find a lover other than her husband in the city. Not only so, this gesture also amounts to being an audacious subversion of the conventional plot of most romantic fiction, turning it upside down. As we know, most love stories often end with clichés like a marriage and a promise for the couple's being "happy ever after". Here, the end of the story that is happily endorsed by patriarchal ideology becomes an unsettlingly new beginning of another story, the beginning of a woman's announcement of her imminent betrayal of her man.

This deliberate, purposely subversion on the part of a liberated woman finds its further proof in her dismissive attitude towards the book that she reads on the train to the city. For her, that book, very possibly one of the popular romantic novels of the day, fails to sustain her interest, for she has already guessed its ending. She needs some other books, other stories that are open-ended, full of interesting adventures and quests. Although no other book is mentioned later in the story, her own quest for the ideal partner, both bodily and mentally, arguably constitutes as a special way of "writing" new stories other than the one she has to read, namely authentic women's stories.

Tentative Rewriting of Women's Plot of Love and Lust through the Agency of Transgressive Sexuality

As a site of "elsewhere" other than the place she usually lives (very possibly a rural area where the author herself lives), the city offers the unnamed woman infinite lures and fascinations with its sights and sounds, including its hotel rooms with wonderful views, its crowd of city dwellers, its dazzling shopping centre full of novelties, and its highly seductive music. In fact, it is exactly a jukebox song called "The Ballad of Lucy Jordan" that lures her into a pub, the site of her imminent life-transforming extramarital affair.

In the pub, an ambiguous place both public and private, the gaudily-dressed woman encounters the other party of the affair, an unnamed man who is certainly a total stranger to her. This somewhat exotic man spontaneously and actively offers words of pleasantries to her, and soon gets into an energetic narration of his own life story, especially highlighting his loneliness and his desperate need for a lover. Even when he is told about the woman's marital status, he is still willing to invite her to play a game called pool. Since the woman does not know how to play this game, the man patiently teaches her about it. After it, the man suggests a walk together, during which he invites her to his home, where he promises to cook for her.

This promise, albeit not a weighty matter at that, does give the woman a sense of untold pleasure that rarely comes in her own life. Back in her own home, it is taken for granted that she, as a woman and a wife, is assigned the task of all the household chores, cooking included. She has never known, or even realised what it is like for a man to cook for her.

After buying a trout, the man swiftly leads the woman out of the city to the place where he lives. It is a seedy and neglected place indeed: located on the top floor of a block of flats, with plain walls, dusty sills, with no valuables whatsoever. Especially noteworthy is the marked absence of any means of communication with the outside world, or any sign indicating the man's past.

For the woman, the apparent discomfort in staying here does not mean much. If she did particularly care about it, she would not have left her home in the first place. What she sees is the possibility for asserting her true self in this completely new place, in her interaction with this completely new man.

The sight of a big cast-iron tub in the bathroom piques her interest, arousing a strong desire in her to get a bath there. This is both symbolic and erotic: both as a ritual to cleanse her old self and as a daring enough invitation for the man's intimacies.

To her great delight, the man seems gentlemanly indeed, unlike most men who make her feel threatened. He carefully and lovingly washes her body, rinses her off, and wraps her in a towel. Even in combing her hair, the man still remembers to praise her blond hair, and stresses women's need to be looked after.

The caring words and behaviours excite in the woman an unquenchable need to explore him through his naked body, "a novelty"① (7)

---

① Claire Keegan, *Antarctica* (New York: Grove Press, 1999). Subsequent citations to this work are given as parenthetical page references in the text.

in her eyes. She even compares herself to Columbus who explores America. Even in lovemaking, the woman still holds an upper hand with "surprising strength in bed, an urgency that bruised him" (7) until they fall into sleep.

Arguably, this unusual portrait of a woman in need and in charge of a man is highly subversive in that it reverses the usual pattern of sexual politics in which a woman is gazed at as an object by a man; also in that it is given unapologetically and unashamedly, justifying it as a legitimate, morally unproblematic act.

When they wake up in darkness, the man dutifully takes charge of dinner all by himself, as he used to promise, while she rests on the couch comfortably, freely watching TV programs. She can hear all too clearly the sound of him "chopping vegetables, the bubble of water boiling on the stove" (8). She can also smell the aroma of the delicious food that "drifted through the room" (8). It dawns on her that the generosity of this man is immense, greatly putting her all-demanding husband in the shade. She cannot help imagining herself to live here with him like this all the time. That husband of hers, so unworthy of her remembrance, is almost too naturally left out of her mind.

The sex after dinner proves equally satisfying for the woman, for she feels that the man does not merely satisfy his own physical needs, but tries all his means to please her, just "like a man leasing himself out to her" (10).

To some extent, the woman's accidental and also inevitable encounter with the man tests out the possibility of asserting and maintaining a true, inviolate female self in her interaction with a man. The radical means, namely through the active agency of transgressive sexuality, unsettlingly shows the extent of desperation into which prolonged oppression and repression of an independent female identity has driven a woman.

Ultimate and Unexpected Patriarchal Imprisonment of the Female Body and Will

In contemporary society, patriarchy's oppression of women remains unchanged. However, it has assumed a more subtle, more concealed form. This is exactly the case with the latter part of the story, where the "generous period" (10) man gradually reveals his vicious, sadistic, monstrous side that can hardly be fathomed or detected previously without extra caution.

Retrospectively, signs of the man's capacity for evil deeds do present themselves on many occasions, which the woman, bent on adventures, is not alert enough to notice. For instance, the meeting place for the woman and him is Gothic enough: apparently a pub, yet described as "a converted prison with barred windows and a low, beamed ceiling" (2) If this is not ominous enough, the beheading of the trout "that looked like it was still alive" (4) is indeed a shocking scene, symbolically foreboding the doom of the woman who used to be equally "alive".

The marked dangerousness of the man first appears when the woman temporarily leaves the man's flat so as to check out of her hotel. In the lobby, she calls home in its telephone booth, only to feel someone behind her. This someone is no other than the man, who, obviously in an accusatory tone, asks her why she "sneaked off" (11) without saying goodbye to him. This certainly forms a marked contrast to his previous "generosity".

However, the man soon follows his highly-charged words "sneak off" with "to lunch and get drunk?" (11), as if he is simply playing a joke on her. This allays the fear in her, who willingly goes to lunch with him, unaware of the change in him.

The second time the man shows his dangerous side occurs when he takes the woman for a walk after lunch. His grip on her is no longer gentle, loving, or kind, but tight enough to hurt her, as is typical of a sadist and controlling freak. Even when the woman blames him for his rudeness, he only loosens his hand, without the least intention to apologise, utterly unlike the man he used to be.

During the walk which increasingly becomes silent and forced, the man starts to tell more specifically about his past failed marriage to a woman and his self-claiming victory for surviving without her presence for one year. The "strange smile" (13) certainly shows his perverted mind at this time—for a man who suffers and cannot recover from a failed love, his potential for destruction, the object of which may be any woman who looks like his old lover in any way, may be unfathomable and shocking enough.

This destructive urge bursts out when they walk deep into the woods, ironically a typical site for both romance and murder. Like an untamed beast, he pushes the woman's back hard against a tree, almost in a gesture of rape. Again and again, he demands, or orders the woman to "say you won't forget me" (14), which the woman, still not fully aware of the danger lurking, obeys. This is followed by more morbidly despairing caresses on the man's part, only to be interrupted by the woman's reminder of him that she has to leave at six on a train.

The ultimate and most terrifying sadist narrative finally comes when the man invites her to his place for the last time as a parting gift. Partly out of gratitude for his onetime generosity, and partly out of a kind wish to console him for her imminent and inevitable departure, she unwittingly follows him there. Lying on his bed, the woman is no longer in the mood for sex with this very man, with merely a sense that it is better to bring the ritual of adultery to a perfect and peaceful closure. However, the man unexpectedly produces from a drawer something that jingles—handcuffs. Before she is fully conscious of the dangerous situation she is suddenly thrown into, her wrists have already been bound to the bed, which the sadist man believes will appeal to her. As if this is still not morbid enough, the man goes into the kitchen to scramble eggs before returning soon enough to feed her in quiet coercion. The juxtaposition of the confining handcuffs with the smell of the food is jarring enough, which seems to imply their homogeneity in nature, both serving as the double-faced man's means of control. After being forced to take the food and drink as the man demands, the woman is drugged to sleep, only to wake up with the discovery that she is both bound and gagged. Despite her pleading with her eyes, the man feels no remorse for what he has done, even claiming it to be an act of love which she will surely understand.

After the man's unexpected departure, albeit obviously only temporarily, the woman attempts to undo the handcuffs with all her strength, only to find the struggle to be in vain. They are bound too tightly to the bed, utterly beyond her powers. Neither can she yell for help, for she cannot chew through the gagging cloth, either. The only chance for her salvation, albeit equally slim, lies in the window, which the man has left open. However, the increasingly cold wind blowing from outside gradually numbs her, who is still naked. The dulled anger in her gradually gives way to the highly existential fear that she may silently die here, in this man-made, out-of-nowhere prison, without any possibility of seeing her husband and children any more.

One of the last visions in her mind before she loses consciousness is Antarctica, which is highly symbolic of the initially promising and yet eventually ill-fated journey that the woman has gone through. As a continent that is full of natural resources and still not fully explored by human beings due to its extremely cold temperature, Antarctica certainly lures them, and feeds their imagination for adventures and new possibilities. However, it is by no means a welcome terrain that invites anyone with no differentiation. Instead, it is a terrain hostile and dangerous enough to bring death at any time to a poorly prepared explorer. Just like such an explorer, the daring woman initially does fulfill her feminist agenda by breaking through patriarchal constraints and restraints and doing what she really wants to do as a free, liberated woman. However, the all-pervasive, overwhelmingly powerful, and highly deceptive patriarchal mechanism of control still manages to ensnare, entrap, and silence her in the end. This tragic ending is indeed one that both the woman and most readers can hardly predict. However, it is a truthful and ethical portrait of the all-too-real dilemmas women still face in contemporary society.

Chapter 3 Making Connections among Unconnectable Fellow Women: Reading Nora Nadjarian's "Exhibition" (Cyprus)

Among all contemporary Cypriot women who write fiction in English, Nora Nadjarian (1966 –) is certainly a very notable one, having won prizes or been commended in international competitions, including the Commonwealth Short Story Competition and the Binnacle International Ultra-Short Competition at the University of Maine at Machias. Her best-known works often centre on such themes as the Cyprus partition of 1974, identity and loss in a highly literary style that features highly concentrated, concise, and precise use of language.

In "Exhibition", one of her most recent short stories, Nadjarian manages to turn an exhibition in a relatively narrow setting (a seemingly small event) into a large, stage-like world of psychological dramas where various female figures, including the female artist and her female audiences gradually reveal to the readers the secret, hidden, unspeakable stories of themselves, of their beloved and lost ones, either by means of "telling" or "showing"[①] when they come face to face with the exhibited items. Through this ritualistic act of shared viewing, the seemingly unconnected and unconnectable fellow women are

① Both "telling" and "showing" are narrative techniques that are fully discussed in Wayne Booth's most-recognized book, *The Rhetoric of Fiction*.

unexpectedly connected as a whole.

Exhibition as a Personal Means of Emotional Catharsis and Artistic Self-expression

For the female artist, the exhibition, first and foremost, holds a highly personal meaning for her: through the public display of her personal things as exhibited items, she manages to give vent to her hidden, repressed feelings for those who are irretrievably lost and yet still haunt her in her memories, namely her father and her mother.

For instance, the suitcase on exhibition carries all the hopes and expectations of her father for her. The sight of it can instill the most powerful encouragement into the female artist for her future pursuit, even conjuring up a hallucination of her father.

The bed on exhibition, however, carries back her not-so-nice memories of her mother. It is exactly on this bed that her mother used to sleep and was discovered to be a whore. Her contradictory double identities as both a mother and a whore has greatly troubled and traumatised her artist daughter for all these years. Through the public display of the highly symbolic bed (a site of shame), however, the artist daughter declares her will to bravely look the past traumatic memory in the face, thus achieving her personal salvation and the possibility to start anew in life.

A less immediate, if not more powerful reason for the female artist's exhibition arises from her strong desire to find the best way to express her artistic self. Despite the apparent ordinariness and even triviality of the exhibited items (some of them belong to the artist herself, while others are randomly found everywhere by her), they serve as very important inspirations for the artist, who is now mentally unbalanced by the demands of her highly demanding trade and needs to make an asymmetrical sculpture exactly based on all these seemingly common, raw, and yet natural (not artificial) materials.

Exhibition as a Means of Female Bonding

If the exhibition merely means something to the female artist, it is sufficient for her to make a private one. The public nature of the exhibition, however, reveals the artist's wish to make connections with others, namely her audiences by reminding them of their past memories and inspiring their deepest, forgotten longings.

Significantly, the audience members (at least mentioned in the text) are all women, revealing the gender of her implied and intended audience: a woman writer ("I"), a whore, an expectant mother, symbolising all possible types of women—respectively the professional woman just like the artist, the often despised "fallen" woman, and the domestic woman. However, all of them are equal (at least contingently) before the exhibition, and have every right to view the exhibited items that mean much to themselves.

For the woman writer ("I"), the piano stool on exhibition "speaks" to her of her past days spent with Miss Nina, her formidable and yet deeply loved Russian piano teacher. It is exactly her onetime strict instructions of her in music that contributes to the cultivation of her artistic temperament, which helps her eventually become a writer.

For the whore, the chair on exhibition reminds her of one of her truly loved clients who fails to reciprocate her affection. For the client, this love affair is nothing but business, and the woman is nothing but a whore who sells her body for money, which he is willing to pay. He does not care to know her past stories, nor does he have the least intention to leave his wife for her. For the woman, however, this affair is by no means a mere matter of sex and money. In fact, she wants to tell him "something indecipherable, something meaningless, something desperate about her life"① (389). She desperately refuses to be seen in a reductive way, yet eventually she is reduced to being a body. After all these years, the sight of the chair once again inspires in her an impulse to write "her autobiography in her head" (389), recording her own "history (or her-story)" that may still be excluded from the official "History" and yet means much to herself.

For the expectant mother, the exhibited items also offer great inspirations. Although none of the items is hers, the act of exhibition itself calls back her own impulse to arrange and rearrange her own private exhibitions—five photos taken in Italy, which carry important messages of love for the man who impregnates her. She wants her unborn child to know about herself, her father, and their mutual love.

Through this highly ritualistic act of shared viewing in the exhibition space, the female artist unexpectedly and yet meaningfully manages to connect the seemingly unconnected and unconnectable fellow

---

① Aleksandar Hemon, ed., *Best European Fiction 2011* (Champaign and London: Dalkey Archive Press, 2010). Subsequent citations to this work are given as parenthetical page references in the text.

women (who do not know each other in actual life) together as a whole. Although their individual stories may vary, they still resemble each other in that their memories and longings that are inspired by the exhibition all arise from their unmistakable nature as women.

Chapter 4 In Defiance of the Confining Law of the Islamic Father: Reading Elif Shafak's *The Bastard of Istanbul* (Turkey)

"A brave and passionate novel" ——Paul Theroux

"Shocking, ambitious, exuberant" ——*Observer*

Elif Shafak (1971 –), the highly acclaimed Turkish Writers' Union Prize winning Turkish novelist, has become one of the most distinctive feminist voices in contemporary Turkish and world literature in English, with her careful infusion of magical-realist fictional techniques with big, important ideas especially concerning the living conditions and fate of contemporary women.

In *The Bastard of Istanbul*, her best known novel to date, she offers a shocking narrative of several generations of Turkish women in a family in Istanbul, as well as its only living male expatriate whose life, both historically and realistically, intertwines with an Armenian family. Despite Shafak's (a bit overly) attention to almost every single voice in these two families, the daring and ultimately profound voice of a central heroine still manages to shine through—Zeliha Kazanzi.

Throughout the narrative, this heroine, who grows from an untamed girl to an increasingly strong-willed woman, constantly surprises and shocks almost everyone in this conventional Muslim neighbourhood in Istanbul. Specifically, the shock comes in many forms. For instance, utterly unlike a feminine girl who obediently follows the written and unwritten rules of female prudence, she puts on an ostentatious miniskirt, wears a nose ring, and carefully shaves her leg with a razor instead of waxing it like others. For her, this simply shows her due admiration for her beautiful body, which is nothing wrong. Her favourite music also shows her different leanings: the artistically exquisite music of a banned transsexual singer. Not only so, she also directly voices her strong will to differ, announcing that she will do whatever she likes to do despite (or because of) hostile interventions from all sides.

This gesture of sheer defiance is by no means a void signifier that comes out of nowhere, but a natural, gradual, and almost inevitable response after many years of patriarchal oppression in Zeliha's family. From her girlhood, she, together with her mother and other siblings, has to obey all demands (both reasonable and unreasonable) from Levent Kazanzi, her authoritarian father. In a sense, the laws of the Muslim DAD function just like the holy *Koran*, standing no objections or questionings, and governing every moment of their lives. For Zeliha, this oppressive atmosphere in the family is indeed repressive enough, no matter in her father's repeated scoldings, his regular spankings, his predinner inspections, or his forbiddance of all family members' due privacy. What infuriates Zeliha more is the marked, deliberate contrast between her father in domesticity and in public. In the neighbours' eyes, this easily angered, highly disciplinary, and easily punitive father successfully masks himself as a good, kind, and loving man that has internalised all the good moral teachings of Islam. This hypocrisy is certainly beyond Zeliha's tolerance. However, confronted with such a powerful father whose patriarchal ideology has a lasting impact on both the family members and the neighbours, the still young Zeliha is powerless for any rebellious act, standing no chance for triumph.

The father's unexpected early death from a family curse that seems to be a magical revenge from the dead Armenians killed by Turks in the 1915 genocide, soon brings an end to the all-pervasive patriarchal rule in the Kazanzi family. However, the temporary absence of the actual father soon gives way to its continuation in other forms: Gulsum, Levent's wife, becomes the matriarch of the family, governing the family in a way no less like her husband. What's more, Mustafa, the only living male in the family, is also eager to assert his role as the rightful heir to the patriarchy. As the only one who disobeys this new, albeit fundamentally still the same rule, Zeliha inevitably becomes the target for their attacks. Gulsum constantly and viciously accuses her daughter of being a whore simply because she dresses, acts and speaks differently from others. Compared to Gulsum's slander in words, Mustafa resorts to both physical violence and verbal attacks in his attempt to put his sister under his control. After a fierce quarrel that is followed by slapping, biting, and punching from both parties, he violently, almost uncontrollably rapes her, which contributes to her untimely pregnancy with a child. When she realises this grim consequence of the unexpected incestuous incident, she has to look hard for a doctor for an abortion all by herself. However, due to the doctor's inability to perform the operation in Zeliha's unquenchable screaming, Asya, the unblessed child, is eventually born out of wedlock without anyone knowing her real father, thus becoming a bastard of Istanbul.

Despite the loss of a good reputation that is of great importance for a woman in the Muslim neighbourhood, Zeliha shows a rare capacity for recovery from her unspeakable and unspoken trauma. When labelled time and again as a family disgrace by Gulsum, she learns to ignore it, for she knows there is no way to reveal the truth (Mustafa has already been sent to America to dodge the family curse) to anyone. When ridiculed by others, she remains equally undaunted, neither accepting the fault found in her nor revealing anything that may pique their further interest in gossiping.

Zeliha also shows a startling capacity for resilience as a strong-willed, spiritually independent woman all over again. Instead of hiding herself indoors as an invisible domestic woman free from humiliations outside, she even goes out all by herself to pursue a public career of her own by opening a tattoo parlour, not to mention her persistence in wearing an outrageously short skirt and even more outrageously high heels. Being a professional woman itself is still not highly expected in the traditional Muslim neighbourhood in Istanbul, not to mention her low status as a disgraced woman. In spite of all the obstacles, Zeliha still manages to do what she wants to do, and persists in doing it, thus achieving independence both spiritually and financially.

Not only being a daring, independent woman herself, she also exerts a subtle and yet unmistakable influence on other members of her family, especially Asya, her illegitimate and yet highly intelligent daughter. Despite her confusion for being told to call her mother "aunt" instead of "mother", as well as the shame in her to see her mother so outlandishly different from others, she secretly, unconsciously, and gradually learns to adore, respect, and even worship her for the rare trait in her mother—the desire and the audacity to be her true self, to be free. This can be seen in no other than her sceptical agnosticism despite the influence of so many highly religious women around her in her formative age, which is unmistakably inherited from her mother, whose lack of religiosity and lack of respect for the FATHER is at least partially caused by her sufferings from her patriarchal father and brother. What's more, contextually speaking, Zeliha's secret endorsement of Asya's attempt to smoke, one of the things forbidden to a Muslim woman, also helps shape her understanding of what liberty means for a woman. When she finally gets to know the truth of her birth, it increasingly dawns on her that her mother is indeed a great and yet undiscovered heroine, for she, albeit in great difficulty, manages to protect the family honour from being tainted by concealing the terrible deeds committed by her brother and bearing all the ensuing troubles and humiliations alone without shedding a single tear.

Not only subtly shaping her own daughter into an equally liberated woman, Zeliha is also secretly admired by Petite-Ma, the most senior member of the house, who unexpectedly picks her (instead of Banu, the highly religious clairvoyant and soothsayer) out as the successor of the family secret of lead pouring, which is believed to be capable of cracking whatever evil eye that might have clustered around a person. Although Petite-Ma's choice of a non-believer for such a highly religious ritual surprises everyone including Zeliha, she does have her reasons: for her, Zeliha is by no means the black sheep in the family. Instead, the underestimated good, such as determination, spirit, and fury in her makes her an ideal choice, the right person for this inheritance. Although Zeliha eventually declines this offer by choosing to stand on her own ground as an agnostic, the grandmother's open consent of her undiscovered, unjustly neglected, or deliberately buried virtues does put Zeliha in high relief.

In a sense, this unusual affirmation of Zeliha's virtues on the part of Petite-Ma is a secret affirmation of her own unexplored, unrealised potential for the construction of a fuller female subjectivity. In other words, for Petite-Ma, Zeliha becomes her secret and highly-cherished double that is capable of fulfilling her secret wish to be different, to be defiant, and to be free. During her own time when Turkish women were undergoing a radical transformation in the public sphere, Petite-Ma started to enjoy an unprecedented independence within her own home. With her husband's consent, not only being able to play music (both Russian and Western repertoires) on the piano, she also learned to speak French, write short stories, draw oil paintings, dress herself splendidly, and throw parties, without doing a day of housework. However, when she unwittingly asked questions related to her husband's past, her always loving husband suddenly became a different man, hardly recognisable any longer. This amounts to saying that even her husband, who seems to be so much different from other patriarchal men, is still profoundly influenced by one of the most deeply trenched patriarchal ideologies regarding the two sexes—a man may indeed love a woman like a pet or a child as much as possible, but a woman is never equal enough to ask a man questions, or to have any say regarding his life. When her husband died, this little, brief span of freedom enjoyed by Petite-Ma during his lifetime also died with him, replaced by the utterly patriarchal control of Levent, her stepson who never treated her like a mother. Now, in Zeliha, Petite-Ma finally finds a true heir, not only for the task of lead pouring, but more importantly for the unfulfilled dream shared by all women who have not completely lost their ideals or expectations of themselves.

As an underprivileged woman living in the Islamic world, from her birth, Zeliha Kazanzi is already entrapped, en-caged, and imprisoned by its age-old patriarchal ideologies. However, despite all this, she still manages to realise the need for a radical and real change in Islamic women's living conditions and spiritual life, and helps both others and herself to make all kinds of attempts to make the change possible. Even in defeat, she never shows undue sentimentality or weakness. Such rare traits in her do make her stand out as a heroic, pioneering figure that is by no means inferior to any man, posing severe and very real challenges to a male-dominated regime. It is exactly one of the most important reasons (apart from the daring mention of Armenians' accusations of Turkish butchers in the 1915 genocide) why Elif Shafak, the equally daring author who successfully invents this character, greatly infuriated the Turkish government for touching their sensitive nerves during the publication of this book in its Turkish edition.

Chapter 5 Seeking for a Home of One's Own: Reading Marilynn Robinson's *Housekeeping* (United States)

"So precise, so distilled, so beautiful that one doesn't want to miss any pleasure it might yield." ——*The New York Times Book Review*

"This is not a novel to be hurried through, for every sentence is a delight." ——Doris Lessing

Among all contemporary women novelists working in the United States, Marilynn Robinson (1943–) is undoubtedly a unique presence. So far, she has written only four novels—a relatively meagre output, especially compared to the extremely productive Joyce Carol Oates, another highly conspicuous fellow woman novelist who has published forty novels, as well as a number of plays and novellas, and many volumes of short stories, poetry, and nonfiction. However, every single work of hers is invariably capable of garnering much attention from both critics and common readers. In fact, these works have earned her numerous and highly prestigious national and international prizes, such as the National Humanities Medal, the Pulitzer Prize for Fiction, the Pen/Hemingway Award, the National Book Award, the National Book Critics Circle Award for Fiction, and the Orange Prize for Fiction.

Robinson's appeal first lies in her highly graceful and intelligent language that is rarely found in other writers' works. Not only so, Robinson also manages to bring a highly humanistic and religious strain to her writings in a postmodern age when even the most fundamental values and beliefs are subjected to the most vigorous questionings and doubts. What's more, almost echoing the rise of the third wave of feminism in the United States in the 1980s, she successfully brings the American tradition of female writing to a new height.

Of all her novels, her debut *Housekeeping* still offers a very good start for new readers, not least due to its subtle, sincere, and profound investigation into the dynamic, and mutually shaping relationship between the modern female identity and the idea of home.

The Modern Patriarchal Ideology of Home

So far, a host of critics have rightly discussed the Victorian myth of "hearth and home". However, it should be noted that this myth continues in the modern era, subtly and yet unmistakably shaping the thoughts and feelings of contemporary men and women. In a narrow sense, this modern home means a family house. More broadly speaking, it also refers to a town, a city, or even a nation. What they all point to, however, is the sense or reality of settledness, stability, peace, order—certainly an ideal condition for middle-class governance in a modern age.

However, this ideal condition is by no means ideal for everyone. Beneath the surface, this ideology of home is profoundly problematic due to its patriarchal nature. In a narrow sense, the much desired sense or reality of stability and order in a family house is in fact achieved at the cost of the largely unacknowledged and overlooked housekeepers, virtually all of whom are women. More importantly and profoundly, this oppressive and repressive ideology of home subtly and yet unmistakably forces itself onto the construction of female subjectivity and self according to the patriarchal form or pattern, thus depriving women of any chance to shape or maintain an independent and true self.

In *Housekeeping*, the fate of both Ruth's grandmother (Sylvia) and her two great-aunts (Lily and Nona) epitomises the tragedies and dilemmas that a patriarchal society relentlessly and remorselessly imposes on female housekeepers. The former devotes her whole life to the maintenance of the family house that is left by her husband without any complaint, and more than accomplishes this task without a fault. However, after her death, she appears in the obituary merely as the humble wife of her "famous" husband whose sensational death from a terrible derailment hit the headlines years ago. Compared to the widow, what Lily and Nona find in the housekeeping is sheer amazement at and exhaustion from its terrible and endless demands that it can make on a housekeeper. Despite their maternal looks, they are actually maiden ladies who have never been asked or need to do such things. Therefore, when they are obliged to do housekeeping for this bereaved family and take care of Ruth and Lucille, they necessarily feel at a loss and badly equipped. After futile attempts for a spell, they finally realise that they are indeed incapable of bringing one disorder after another back into order. They cannot but hand over this exhausting, frustrating, and fundamentally impossible mission to someone else, who turns out to be Sylvie, the two children's eccentric, remote, vagrant-like aunt. To a large extent, the failure on the two great-aunts' part undoubtedly bears testimony to the fact that it is indeed far from being easy for a woman to maintain a proper house, who has to devote no less energy and wisdom to it than that of a career man or woman.

The Female Introduction of Radically New Ways of Housekeeping

Faced with the numerous patriarchal expectations and requirements for housekeeping, a traditional, unenlightened female housekeeper often has to decide between the following two options: either to choose complicity with patriarchy (such as the grandmother Sylvia), or helplessly escape from it (such as Lily and Nona). However, with the increasing consciousness of a distinctly female subjectivity that refuses to be otherised or objectified by patriarchy, more and more domestic women manage to introduce brand new ways of keeping the house so as to liberate themselves from a narrow, circumscribed way of life, and to make the house really their own.

In H*ousekeeping*, Sylvie, the newly-arrived aunt of the two children, in more than one sense, does neatly belong to the critics' carefully made category of "New American Eve"① . In fact, the very selection of her (a vagrant long away from home), not anyone else, as the successor to this "proper" "father-house"② is itself an "improper" choice. It is practically inevitable that she will bring something

① Maureen Ryan, "Marilynne Robinson's *Housekeeping*: The Subversive Narrative and the New American Eve," *South Atlantic Review*, 56, no. 1 (1991), 86.

② It should be noted that even in the absence of an actual father figure, he still exerts a palpable influence on his female family members with his "absent presence".

new, unexpected, and unconventional to this house.

The changes brought about by this aunt are indeed tremendous. For Sylvie, the traditional way of housekeeping is simply meaningless and boring, excluding many interesting possibilities that she used to experience and enjoy in her vagrant life. Therefore, she replaces it with a radically new way of housekeeping that blurs the sharp and clear-cut boundary between outside and inside, between the human world and nature. For instance, in Sylvie's notion, the kitchen window and the trapdoor are no longer symbols of confinement or separation, but linking points, thresholds that are open to a larger world. In fact, besides the kitchen window and the trapdoor, every other part of the house is equally inviting to the outside world: the leaves freely gather in the corners, the crickets cry in the pantry, the squirrels play in the eaves, the sparrows sing in the attic. Even the flood that comes when the lake waters rise is not seen as a life-destroying force, but simply a natural phenomenon—all Sylvie and the children have to do is to stay on the second floor and patiently wait for it to subside. When the light shines into the house, it is the day; when it is dark, the house should also remain in the dark, with no use for modern electrical alliances.

To many conventional people, this kind of housekeeping amounts to "de-housekeeping" or "un-housekeeping". One critic even argues that "slowly demolishing the children's home, Sylvie completely ignores their longing for normalcy"① . Such an interpretation seems to

---

① Maria Moss, "The Search for Sanctuary: Marilynne Robinson's *Housekeeping* and E. Annie Proulx's *The Shipping News*," *Amerikastudien/American Studies*, 49, no. 1 (2004), 83.

be too simplistic or too "realistic", missing the most significant message the text attempts to convey. This kind of housekeeping may be unorthodox, but its unorthodoxy exactly and fundamentally deconstructs the patriarchal conventions and ideologies that have long suffocated and confined female housekeepers, and offer a highly symbolic, non-patriarchal alternative to the so-called standard.

Redefinition of the Meaning of "Home"

For many people, especially under the pervasive influence of various patriarchal instructions and persuasions, the "home" means a fixed entity, no matter it is a family house, a town or city, or a nation. The problem with it is the hegemonic power inherent in its very naming or definition, which is made "by" men and "for" men alone. For modern women, especially those who get a chance to experience the world outside mere domesticity, a "home" should be a fluid, unfixed, dynamic, non-oppressive, liberating space/site, or to be exact, a "shelter" in the psychological sense. As long as it can bring a sense of security in women, it can be rightfully counted as a home.

In *Housekeeping*, Sylvie certainly represents the most daring type of female namer of a "home" in the modern world. Apart from introducing an utterly radical way of housekeeping for the conventional house, she also introduces to the children, especially the more sympathetic Ruth, quite a few alternatives that are equally called "home". For instance, they often go to the woods for communion with nature. For them, this natural world provides no less sense of security and peace than their own "civilised" home. Besides, they also build makeshift shelter there for their nightly stay. Most importantly, a highly dramatised separation experience in the woods drives home to them the most profound meaning of home—the so-called home is not a physical place (be it the conventional family house, the woods, or a makeshift shelter), but a psychological site, an imaginary, invisible and yet unmistakably present, quasi-religious presence. As long as one keeps her most dear family members by their side or in their hearts, one certainly has a home of his/her own.

Such transient or vagrant experiences that are highly engaged with "elements of Emersonian transcendentalism"① are highly meaningful in that they are good and active experiments to construct different, alternative forms of home. In a sense, this life-style is indeed "drifting". However, what Sylvie and the children are drifting away from is not "home", but the conventional and restrictive notion of "family house" as the only legitimate and reasonable "home" for a domestic woman.

The Female Dilemma in Constructing a non-Patriarchal Home in a Patriarchal World

Arguably, both the radically new ways of housekeeping and redefinition of a home on the part of modern women have severely shaken (if not toppled) the foundation of patriarchal rules and regulations. The

---

① Maggie Galehouse, "Their Own Private Idaho: Transience in Marilynne Robinson's *Housekeeping*," *Contemporary Literature*, 41, no. 1 (2000), 118.

patriarchal authorities certainly cannot allow the women to have their own way. Therefore, an intervention, direct or indirect, is bound to occur.

This is exactly the case with *Housekeeping*. The first one to defect from Sylvie is Lucille, Ruth's sister. When she grows up, she increasingly feels that she actually belongs to the other world (the patriarchal world), not this new world of Sylvie's making. Therefore, she eventually abandons her aunt and sister for another highly symbolic house—the house of her home economics teacher (someone who is supposed to be an expert in conventional housekeeping).

After Lucille's defection, more severe interventions from the town people quickly ensue. Among them are the sheriff (a symbol of law and regulation), and the good churchgoing women of Fingerbone (a symbol of public opinion). Together, they threaten to bring an end to Sylvie's unconventional housekeeping, and more menacingly, to take Ruth away from Sylvie, who is believed to be incapable of taking care of children and even making them stray from the right path.

Confronted with such overwhelmingly powerful and unsympathetic accomplices of patriarchy, the contingently powerless Sylvie makes one of her most daring decisions—to burn down the family house. For some feminist critics, this radical gesture is utterly necessary and promising, for it cuts the last link (or cuff) that bonds Sylvie and the town, and finally pushes Sylvie and Ruth to cross the highly symbolic and largely forbidden railway bridge once and for all, so as to lead a thoroughly vagrant, transient, and inherently free life in the woods, without needing to fall victim to the surveillance and watchful gazes from the town people. Symbolically speaking, this is certainly a viable choice.

However, to interpret this act merely from an overly feminist perspective is still reductive, for it is not intended by Sylvie (in fact, she is forced to do so), nor utterly endorsed by Ruth (she often imagines Lucille to be in their family house in her post-civilised life) . The life they really intend to lead is in fact a double life—both leading an unconventional, interesting and emotionally rewarding life in their conventional house, and leading a complimentary, alternative life in their unconventional homes in nature. All the time, they have tried to balance the two lives by two means of housekeeping. What these two kinds of "home" and "housekeeping" have in common is the sense of security that arises from their mutual love, care and other kinds of emotional nourishment for each other. To safeguard this most important "home", they have to destroy the physical family house—certainly one of their treasured homes despite their great reluctance. This undoubtedly bears testimony to modern women's dilemma in trying to construct a non-patriarchal home in a patriarchal world. Compared to others, they have to pay a much heavier price for their sheer difference.

Chapter 6 In Search of the Traumatic Past for Reshaping the Present Female Identity: Reading Alice Munro's "Differently" (Canada)

"Munro's stories possess almost all the things a reader might desire—anecdotes, shining everyday details, sexual passion, family history, quirky characters, new landscapes, humor, wisdom."

——*Philadelphia Inquirer*

"Brilliant... [Munro is] an unrivalled chronicler of human nature."

——*The Sunday Times*

As a celebrated Canadian writer of short stories who won the highly-coveted Nobel Prize for Literature in 2013, Alice Munro (1931–) frequently goes far beyond readers' horizon of expectations by managing to mine her familiar and seemingly ordinary milieu, place and people for their largely unfamiliar and extra-ordinary sides. This is exactly the case with her 1990 collection *Friend of My Youth*, especially "Differently", in which Munro offers Georgia, her heroine an opportunity for a purposeful re-investigation into her own troubled past that has constantly haunted her present life with its lies, secrets and silences, so as to see life "differently". What she especially seeks to find out are those episodes of her past connected to Maya, her onetime friend and eventually unforgivable arch-rival.

Unexpected Female Bonds in the Patriarchal Space

For domestic women who are denied opportunities for their own careers, public space outside their homes is often still an "othering", patriarchal place where they largely feel ill at ease. However, once within such space, some highly perceptive women do get a glimpse of the possibility of an alternative life they may lead, an alternative self they may fashion themselves into.

This is exactly what happens to Georgia, the reminiscent heroine in Munro's "Differently". During a party thrown by a rich heiress named Maya, she reluctantly follows Ben, her husband as well as others simply for the sake of social formality. In fact, from a young age, Georgia has formed a low opinion of those wealthy girls, believing them to be "spoiled and brainless" (223)[①]. Despite the moral rigidity and its reductive tendency from today's standards, her view on wealth and those people with it indeed has a certain truth about it in her own times. Therefore, when she first meets Maya, the hostess of the party and the immensely rich girl, she is struck by the apparent incongruity and incompatibility of her looks, clothing and airs with her "rich" status—what she sees is a girl "barefoot, wearing a long shapeless robe of coarse brown cloth that looked like burlap" (224), with her hair "almost the same dull-brown color as the robe" (224), her skin "rough and pale, with marks like faint bird tracks in the hollows of her

---

① Alice Munro, *Friend of My Youth* (New York: Vintage Books, 1991). Subsequent citations to this work are given as parenthetical page references in the text.

cheeks" (224). This unadorned and thus natural side of Maya, together with her "arrogant and indifferent" (224) airs, impresses Georgia greatly. She feels all this both "disconcerting, and wonderful" (224). For a girl used to seeing conventional ways and conventional people, the shock goes without saying. What follows the shock, however, is a strong revelation of what a daring, independent (both financially and mentally) girl of her age can possibly be.

Besides Maya's unconventional presence, Georgia is also drawn to her because of her perceptive discovery of her profound sadness as the party approaches its end. Although she has not yet seen Maya as her double, she does see through the unacknowledged and overlooked fact that "she doesn't love him (Maya's husband)" (226), thus sympathising with her for her secret sufferings in marriage.

Such sympathies soon develop into female bonds on two levels—friendship as wives, and more as themselves. Besides the time they can spend together in the presence of their husbands during family dinners, they can also exchange their private thoughts and feelings with each other in their absence—over coffee, in each other's kitchens, which, at least for a moment, are no longer their husbands' exclusive domain.

Or they can simply go to places other than their own homes during lunch time, namely the Moghul's Court, a seedy, grandiose bar in a large, grim railway hotel, and a hippie restaurant on Blanshard Street. Both places are highly symbolic: the former place carries with it an exotic flavour that seems to offer some haven for their escape from the mundane everyday life, while the latter seems to be full of carnivalesque potentialities. Indeed, it is exactly there that the two women start to perform their newly-forged, self-fashioned identities, such as a widow who has served with their husbands in various outposts of the Empire, a grumpy, secretly socialistic hired companion named Miss Amy Jukes, or refugees from a commune.

Apart from these games, these places also serve as free space where they can really talk about anything about themselves, including their past and their present, temporarily free from men's interventions. It is during such intimate exchanges that they reveal, for the very first time, to each other that they feel increasingly weary of and discouraged by their husbands, who rigidly model themselves after the "ideal" man and also expect them to follow the stereotype of an "ideal" woman. The daring Maya goes on to reveal her current secret extramarital affair with Harvey, as well as her even earlier elopement with a musician before this affair. For her, the affair this time is mere exercise, while the earlier one is her only true and desperate attempt for love. However, both affairs bring more satisfaction to her life than her encumbering marriage.

Unexpected Awakening of Female Desire

For Georgia, Maya's daring introduction to a new system of discourse both in language and body indeed comes as a great shock that definitively jolts her out of her usual being as a mere wife in her husband's house. She is suddenly aware of a strong need for a true "room of her own" —the bookstore, where she gets a part-time job, as well as her own way of life. There she can both support herself financially and meet those people who are willing to talk to her about their favourite books. She does prove to be good for the job, being much liked and appreciated for her energy, her wit, and her ideas. When the store is empty of any customers, she can equally feel at ease, for the calm that comes with the emptiness enables her to watch the street outside "in a finely balance and suspended state" (231).

It is in the bookstore that Georgia sees a stranger's appealing reflection in the glass. His profile, his pallor, his hair, and his way of moving brings out something hidden in her, namely—female desire. Once inside, this stranger, by the name of Miles, actively engages her into conversations by telling her things about himself and showing her various pictures. After piquing her interest, he leaves without informing her of it, only to return another evening, telling more fantastic tales. Just as the narrator comments, "(b)y attention and avoidance, impersonal conversations in close proximity, by his oblivious prowling, and unsmiling, lengthy, gray-eyed looks, he soon had Georgia in a disturbed and not disagreeable state." (232)

With Miles' seduction, Georgia, the sexually inexperienced and psychologically immature woman as she is, cannot help being drawn to him, in an obviously fatal manner. When he eventually offers her a ride on his motorcycle to the beach, she instinctively knows what will happen, and decides to let it so. In the imperfect shelter of some broombushes, she completes the ritual of being a mistress. When she walks back home after lovemaking, she feels herself as "a strengthened and lightened woman, not in the least in love, favored by the universe" (232).

The awakening of her real sexual desire and the knowledge of what she really wants in a man, finally make lovemaking no longer "a chore" (228), but an act that empowers her greatly. From this moment on, she is no longer the old self again, but two selves, with one remaining as the ideal wife fulfilling her duties, and the other (long forgotten) satisfying her own long-repressed desires. From this moment on, she has two maps of the city in her mind, with one guiding routes to those usual places she is obliged to visit, and the other guiding routes she alone knows—to those temporary hiding places where she and Miles can make love in secret.

Spiritual Epiphany in the Contexts of Male Humiliation and Female Betrayal

For those women only recently aware of their own needs, transgressive acts like adultery can be both liberating and unnerving. This is indeed the case with Georgia. Despite her sense of happiness in her indulgence in the passion generated by Miles' seductive eyes and hands, she is still not free from moral guilt, constantly doubting herself for her unfaithfulness to her husband. She cannot help watching other women for any signs of similar transgression, as if any discovery of such a possibility may well reassure her and make her feel no different from others. She also feels uneasy for her constant lies to others when she needs to find Miles for sex.

Besides the self-doubt cast on her affair with Miles, Georgia also witnesses in person the changes that occur to Miles. From the very beginning, his explicit or implicit demand for the utterance of love on her part seems ominous. In fact, this utterance is "defining, inflating, obscuring whatever it was they did feel" (233), as if their love for each other may well disappear without such verbal confirmations.

Unfortunately, later encounters between Georgia and Miles only test out the truth of her ominous feelings. During one night in Clover Point, their usual dating place, Miles finally reveals his sadistic and perverted nature by suggesting a quartet in lovemaking, including Ben (Georgia's husband) and Laura (Miles' wife). This outrages and bitterly strikes Georgia, who believes it to be utterly disgusting. However, the lecherous Miles continues to fondle her, as if he feels that Georgia's offense is only a necessary pretence for further flirtations. After recognising Georgia's firm refusal to comply with his demands, his caresses become violent, just as his words become highly abusive, calling her bad names.

Such onslaughts, both verbal and physical, shock Georgia into recognition of what her "liberating" affair really is. Compared with Ben, her husband, Miles is indeed sexually attractive. However, beneath the skin, he is the same as Ben, for both represent the all-pervasive patriarchal order that necessarily reduces women to an inferior status of being "gazed at" and "controlled". In their eyes, she is by no means a subject like them, either becoming their victims or being complicit with them. If she intends to find her own voice and expects him to respect her, she is subjected to humiliations and accusations.

Such shocking recognition of patriarchy's hidden nature does not end as Georgia's only epiphany, for she is soon struck by another equally unsettling revelation: the (possibly unconscious) betrayal of Maya, her best friend. During the wait for Miles' call, Georgia unexpectedly receives one from Maya, who volunteers to persuade Miles to apologise to Georgia for his highly inappropriate words and behaviours.

However, throughout the sleepless night, the impatient and anxious Georgia receives not a single call as a reply. She cannot help fathoming various possibilities as justifications for Maya's non-reply, such as the temporary disorder of Maya's phone, any illness that suddenly strikes Maya, or any accident that may happen to Maya's husband.

However, when Maya's call finally comes, she, with both honesty and shame, reveals to Georgia about her infidelity to her by (probably) having sex with Miles in their conversations about Georgia. This is certainly unbearable for the already traumatised Georgia, who immediately hangs up the phone in a rage. Later, when Maya comes to her door for an apology, Georgia, despite her reluctance, has to let her in. Smoking one cigarette after another, Maya tells her that Miles is definitely not worthy of her love, and hopes that they can patch up after such an incident. Still not recovering from double shocks, Georgia shows no sign of relent by neurotically wiping the floor.

Aware of the havoc wreaked on her friend, the displaced Maya has to leave. But she still insists on making more phone calls to Georgia, who deliberately refuses to answer. Later, she shifts to letter writing, hoping to win Georgia back. If Georgia still refuses to forgive her, she promises to write no more to her, which she does. Besides Maya, Miles also phones Georgia, who also hangs up on him.

For Georgia, such a clear break with both her lover and her friend is "a vengeful pleasure" (241). For a long time, she has merely attached her own self to them, falling "addiction to the gifts of those two pale prodigies" (241), these "slippery, shimmery—liars, seducers, finaglers" (241). Now, she must break away from their explicit or implicit control of her, and shape her own subjectivity.

The very last thing to do before her initiation into her own self-fashioning is nothing short of a surprise to all: leaving Ben. During the painful wait for the call from Maya, it finally dawns on Georgia that she is surrounded by sham, among which the biggest one is her marriage. She no longer expects her married life to drag on endlessly for mere appearances and contrivance, just as she used to at a young age. Therefore, she must decisively bring an end to this self-deceptive institution once for all. After an unabashed confession to Ben about her affair with Miles, she finally divorces him and regains her freedom.

Towards a Renewed Confirmation of the Pursuit of Female Self in Remaking Female Bonds

Decisions, especially daring ones in people's eyes, tend to leave many after-effects, some of which may haunt the decision-maker for a prolonged period. This is the case with Georgia. Despite its profoundly subversive nature, her fierce breakup with her ex-husband and best friend at that time still troubles her till this day. Part of the reason for her taking a creative writing course possibly lies in her unconscious desire to relieve her through words and writing of those things that trouble her and refuse to leave her alone.

Writing alone seems insufficient to heal her past traumatic memories. Neither is the uneventful present life on a farm in Ontario with her writing instructor hereafter enough to overcome her troubled past. Instead of simply erasing the past, what she really needs to do is to face it squarely and confidently by returning to Victoria where her past lies. Deeply, she is unsure whether she will be welcome there, neither is she certain of what may befall her there, especially taking into consideration the fact that Maya is already dead.

Fortunately, Georgia, although in an uncertain state, embarks on this soul-searching, highly symbolic quest. When she finally arrives at the house of Raymond and Maya, she is surprised to find it all changed. Everything that shows signs of Maya's presence is gone for good, only to be replaced by things belonging to Anne, Raymond's new wife. Raymond is equally changed in looks, although still recognisable.

When Raymond relates to her things about Maya's last days, she inevitably feels touched, especially by the one about the young gardener who tends the garden for her and finally leaves them after the termination of the employment. For the unfeeling Raymond, the fact that the gardener simply leaves without saying goodbye is cold. It is Georgia alone who knows the secret wishes and desires hidden inside the dying Maya's heart. It is also Georgia alone who truly sympathises and identifies with her.

Another thing Raymond regrets over for Maya is her apparent discard for her good enough life and her constant eagerness to seek something else, something more dramatic and more revelatory. In his view, to be happy, one should be contented to be an ordinary person, and leads a simple life. Unlike him, Maya has certainly made a great mistake by being otherwise. Far from persuading Georgia to accept his way, his words only reinforces her in the belief that life, especially that assigned by patriarchy to women, should indeed be lived otherwise— "whatever she did she would have to do again" (242). There is indeed no need for her to feel any remorse for the way she has changed her life. She is right in making her decision at that time, through and through. When Raymond asks her how they should behave if they believe in their imminent death, she jokingly replies with "Differently" (242), although she believes otherwise.

Seen together, these two things related by Raymond undoubtedly resemble each other in two ways: firstly, they are both about Maya, and both are misinterpreted by her husband; secondly, and more importantly, they reawaken in Georgia the long-dormant awareness of her deep bonds with Maya in spite of her (possibly unconscious) betrayal. Only in re-discovering their shared secret wishes, desires, dreams, pains and miseries as fellow women (instead of being endlessly obsessed with the hurts inflicted on her), can Georgia get over her past traumatic memories and manage to lead a really new life from now on.

In her often unsettling and ambiguous portrayals of female relationships, such as that between mother and daughter, between siblings, between female friends (as in "Differently" and other short stories in *Friend of My Youth*), Munro certainly poses profound and utterly relevant questions to both her readers and herself: what connects and separates people, especially those who befriend each other and hold important meanings for each other? If betrayal or hurt is inevitable, can there be any possibility for redemption? Is refusal to forgive also self-damaging? Can we fashion our own self, identity or subjectivity merely by ourselves? No provider of easy answers herself, she does provoke us, time and again in her fiction, into pondering over them and going on a quest for our own selves, just like her heroines. That may well be where her true greatness and charm lie.

Chapter 7 Electra Complex and Its Discontent: Reading Sharon Leach's "All the Secret Things No One Ever Knows" (Jamaica)

Among contemporary Jamaican women writers of fiction in English, Sharon Leach, the Musgrave Bronze Medal awardee from the council of the Institute of Jamaica, indeed merits due critical attention, whose fiction has been widely anthologised in various highly prestigious publications, such as *Kunapipi: Journal of Postcolonial Writing*, *Iron Balloons: Hit Fiction from Jamaica's Calabash Writers' Workshop*, *Stories from Blue Latitudes: Caribbean Women Writers at Home and Abroad*, *the Jamaica Journal*, *Caribbean Writing Today*, *Calabash*, and *Afrobeat*, among others. In "All the Secret Things No One Ever Knows", an outstanding entry from the 2013 Commonwealth Short Story Prize, Leach makes a daring foray into a contemporary Caribbean version of the Electra Complex, a profoundly unsettling, hopelessly complex, impossibly twisted relationship between a Jamaican daughter and her father both psychologically and sexually.

From Political Turmoil to Domestic Chaos

Despite the fast acceleration of globalisation on a worldwide plane, regional strife greatly intensifies instead of diminishing. This is exactly the case with Jamaica, where mounting tensions due to differences in political views often give rise to conflicts and confrontations between the state apparatus and the dissenting groups. In the short story, an uprising downtown in September 1998 effectively epitomises the unsettling political turmoil in Jamaica, which puts everyone, both guilty and innocent, under great risks.

Not only does the political turmoil provide an apt background for many equally chaotic Jamaican households, it also aggravates their situation. In the short story, Raymond, the heroine's father, an owner of a top-rated construction company and the patriarch of a family, harbours double anxieties: not only does he acutely feel himself, a company owner, under the impact of the worsening political situation, he also fears the loss of holding over his family members—his wife (Camille), his two sons (Stephen and James), and his daughter, whom he undifferentiatingly treat as his inviolable private property. Not only does he succeed in containing them financially, he also makes all kinds of attempt to control them physically and emotionally, especially after the all-affecting riot. For instance, the mother, a former Miss Jamaica contestant who goes straight from her mother's house to her husband's, has become so accustomed to his governance that she is virtually a dutiful servant, whose sole aim in life is to win her husband's acknowledgment for her various efforts to please him, such as coordinating dinner and prettifying herself all the time for his gaze. Due to the father's perverted (mis-) guidance, the daughter is even more tied to her father both emotionally and physically. In her mind, her father is not only a father in the conventional sense, but also her boyfriend whose flirty words— "I was the only woman he ever needed"[①] (105) and erotic caresses— "He'd been coming to my room since I was twelve" (111) sooth her and even define her very being. Compared to her mother, she believes that she "would have made a better wife" (111) for her father.

The Daughter's Sudden and Unexpected Awakening of her Plight

For minors who are still incapable of understanding the true meaning of their own sexuality and the degree of intimacy between family members, only unexpected, even shocking discoveries of the truth otherwise than that taught by their parents can alert them to the plight in which they are trapped.

In the short story, the naive daughter truly believes in her father's self-claiming devotion to her, never casting any doubt on it whatsoever. However, during the aforesaid riot, afraid of being left alone in the car, she secretly follows her driver to find her father, only to see a girl of almost her own age slapping her own father hard in the face in a theatrical manner for belated arrival in her besieged beauty salon. Instead of falling into a rage as she expects, her father simply stands there "watching her sadly, like a puppy whose chew toy had been taken away from him" (107). This unexpected sight of another woman's presence in her father's life jolts her out of her foolish, simple and

① *Pepperpot: Best New Stories from the Caribbean* (New York and Leeds: Peekash Press, 2014). Subsequent citations to this work are given as parenthetical page references in the text.

blind belief in her father's incestuous commitment to her and forces her to realise the shocking fact that she is by no means the only one whom her father cares about in that special, highly erotic way. Her self-justified twisted world that is unsettlingly made up by her and her father inevitably crumbles down.

The Daughter's Perverted Sexuality as a Strategy of Retaliation and Self-assertion against Patriarchy

For the still largely powerless minors who believe themselves to have lost the parents' affection, the most direct means to retaliate against them is to deliberately direct their affections towards someone other than them. On the one hand, this is a self-deceptive, but indeed temporarily effective means of asserting the minors' fragile sense of honour. On the other hand, this serves as a loud warning to the parents of their potential loss of their children, forcing them to be re-aware of the children's importance to them.

In the short story, the young daughter does all this and more. After witnessing her father's affair with Mignonette, a girl of almost her own age, she cannot help obsessing over him kissing the girl. In her mind, such kisses should be reserved for no one but herself. This painful fantasy haunts her so much and so relentlessly that she cannot help showing her displeasure openly during a family dinner, especially after she finds that her knowing father still deliberately ignores the blow that his adultery with that girl deals to her.

Not only does the daughter deliberately let her father know her dissatisfaction with him for his "betrayal", she goes even further by openly seducing a policeman called Rick behind her father's back. The reason why Rick is chosen as the daughter's boyfriend simply lies in the secret pleasure such a disobedient act① brings to her. Time and again, she cannot help imagining herself happily violated by him, just as what she imagines her father does with Mignonette.

However, with the unexpected suicide of Stephen, the eldest brother in the father's study, the father feels great unease in approaching his daughter the same way as before, which greatly lets down the lovesick daughter and drives her to drift increasingly apart from him by pretending Rick to be her father and allowing him to take as much liberty with her as he wants, as long as he does not abandon her like her own father. The daughter's displacement of attachment from her biological father to Rick, the surrogate father is further made possible when she, in packing to go to college, opens the letter left by Stephen before his suicide, which reveals its true and alarming cause—his father's despicable sodomy with him (not to mention James and the daughter, who are also sexually abused by him), as well as his father's attempt to make him feel complicit for such an act. When the daughter finally leaves the trauma-ridden Jamaica for Cornell University in the United States, this desperate desire to see a father figure in Rick intensifies (instead of lessening), especially in the wake of the September 11th terrorist attacks which greatly fuel up Americans' hostility towards and phobia for all foreigners. She even maxes out all her credit cards on plane tickets for Rick to see her almost every weekend in the

---

① As a rule, girls in Jamaica are not supposed to date with those people outside their social circle.

United States.

Eventually, the skyrocketing bill for the credit cards makes its effect felt by the enraged father, who knows for certain that her daughter has a lover other than himself. This is exactly what the daughter's love affair intends to bring: his father's displeasure and jealousy, which in turn will bring pleasure and thrill to the daughter. In fact, prior to Rick, she used to date a fellow student called Troy for the same reason, namely arousing his father's jealousy. At that time, her father vowed to kill her in case he should see another boy in her life in the future.

Instead of flying into a rage for her daughter's second "offence", the father reemphasises his timeless devotion to the daughter on the phone: "you mean more to me than my own life...I know you've felt abandoned...but I *love* you" (119). Such a pronouncement does quench the daughter's discontent for a while. However, when they meet later in person, her father's confession to her for his decision to divorce her mother and marry Mignonette finally drives home to her that he comes here not only to inform her of a sad domestic fact concerning her parents, but to tell her that she, instead of her mother, is dumped. The further, more forceful proof of love that is highly expected by the daughter turns out to be a more deadly blow. This infuriates her so much that she cannot help calling her father "a sick piece of shit" (120), only to be returned with a more disgusting reply on the part of her father: "if I am, then what are you?" (120) In a sense, such vicious, humiliating mutual verbal attacks from both parties tellingly show the problematic relationship between the father and the daughter, as well the equally, if not more problematic manoeuvres each of them attempt to make.

The Temporary Halt to Patriarchy and the Anxiety of Its Ghostly Influence

For those children who are used to being emotionally over-attached to their parents, even the parents' bodily and mental injuries on them cannot dispel their deeply-entrenched attachment. Even in their death, they still manage to exert untold influences on their living children, haunting them like a restless ghost.

As can be seen in the short story, in spite of the verbal malice and shamelessness in the father's words, the daughter still uncontrollably yearns for him, and feels unable to imagine a life without him, even with the knowledge that such a longing is utterly unreasonable, and that Rick, instead of her father, is someone who truly merits her devotion. Even after Rick resorts to radical means by shooting the morally reprehensible father to death, the deeply troubled father-daughter problem still remains, for the daughter is still haunted by the presence of the absent father— "I... trying to imagine what the day after tomorrow would be like. But I couldn't. All I could think about was tomorrow, and hope it would be a perfect day for a murder." (123)

Throughout the highly plot-driven narrative, Leach indeed succeeds in bringing to light all the secrets things that happen within a problematic household against an even more problematic backdrop, especially the complex sexual and emotional bonds between the daughter and the patriarchal father, which render the former psychologically twisted, and the latter a demonic figure whose terrifying and undying hold over all his family members is nothing short of a nightmare through and through.

Chapter 8 Ambivalence and Contradictions within Caribbean Motherhood: Reading Jamaica Kincaid's *Annie John* (United States/Antigua & Barbuda)

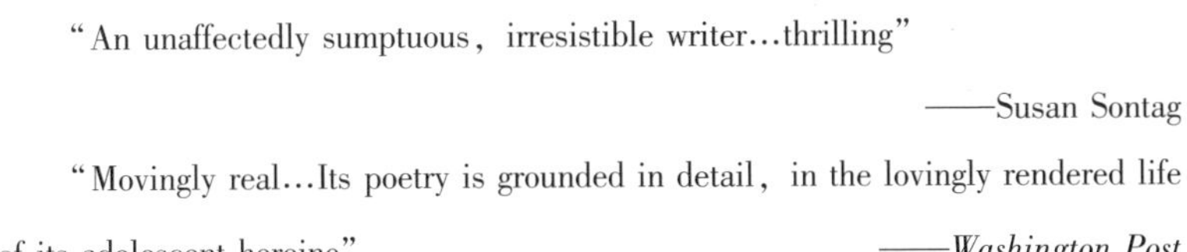

"An unaffectedly sumptuous, irresistible writer...thrilling"

——Susan Sontag

"Movingly real...Its poetry is grounded in detail, in the lovingly rendered life of its adolescent heroine"

——*Washington Post*

Among contemporary women writers from the Caribbean countries, Antigua-born Jamaica Kincaid (1949–) has emerged as one of the most critically acclaimed. Her highly poetic literary style, and her thorough and honest investigation into the post-colonial Caribbean psyche, especially that of her fellow women have become her trademarks. What most sets her apart, however, is her consistent, if not obsessive concern over the mother-daughter relationship. As she herself remarked in her humble way, "I've never written about anyone except myself and my mother. I'm just one of those pathetic people for whom writing is therapy."① It is exactly with the inspiration (albeit not simply autobiographical mimicry) of her own mother-daughter relationship that she manages to mine the complex, contradictory, unsettling, and yet pro-

① Emily Listfield, "Straight from the Heart," *Harper's Bazaar*, 123 (October 1990), 82.

foundly revelatory relationships between various mother figures and daughter figures in her fiction. Apart from *The Autobiography of My Mother*, *Annie John* is undoubtedly a text that best and most fully addresses this subject.

From the very start and throughout the novel, Annie John, the outspoken and active heroine has maintained an inseparable, albeit constantly changing relationship with her mother.

Initially, due to her unusual physical beauty and charm, as is shown in almost every part of her body—her head, neck, hair, nose, mouth, hands, face, figure, and voice, this mother is evidently much idealised as Annie's unrivalled role model. It is especially worth noting that Annie even compares her mother's head to the Queen of England: "Her head looked as if it should be on a sixpence." (18)①

Not only being her most-prized source of pride and joy, Annie's mother also constitutes as the glorious emotional centre in her life. For Annie, the biggest happiness in life lies in being together with her mother. For instance, the mother's loving kisses on her lips and neck, the bath the mother takes with her together, the cooking and washing her mother does for her, the stories they share, combine to make her feel that "It was in such a paradise that I lived" (25).

However, as she grows up, it dawns upon Annie as a massive shock that this same mother has gradually become alienated from her, as if she no longer wishes to love her just like before. For instance, she no longer likes Annie to wear clothes made of the same fabric as hers,

---

① Jamaica Kincaid, *Annie John* (London: Vintage Books, 1997). Subsequent citations to this work are given as parenthetical page references in the text.

neither does she enjoy the time she used to spend with Annie looking through the memory-laden trunk, not to mention her sheer refusal to take baths together with Annie any more. This sudden change in the mother' s attitude toward her turns Annie' s Edenic world upside down— "To say that I felt the earth swept away from under me would not be going too far" (26); "the ground wash out from under" (27) her.

Not only rejecting and slighting her (at least to the extremely sensitive Annie), the same mother even gradually morphs into an oppressive force in her life, constantly disciplining her in a dominant-submissive mode, not by direct, or physical force or violence, but by psychological torture that includes, among other things, contemptuous and humiliating facial expressions (such as curling her lips, casting a watchful and imprisoning gaze), as well as accusatory and vicious language (such as cursing her daughter, calling her "slut") .

The underlying reason for the mother' s abuse of her own daughter largely lies in the various forces that combine to shape her into being their ideal representative. In a sense, the mother represents, or embodies the ideal, albeit actually highly reductive and limiting femininity or womanhood that is directly or indirectly prescribed by colonial (English) and patriarchal ideologies, which include "proper" behaviour and manners, "proper" training and recreations, and "proper" distance for a lady. Internalising all this as a good accomplice, the mother attempts to turn her daughter into such a model young lady. She certainly cannot allow her daughter to grow up otherwise, especially taking into account that she has already sensed her daughter' s potential for rebellion in her early childhood.

However, with the inevitable maturity in both body and mind, coupled with her extreme sensitivity to the people and the world, the gradually awakened daughter learns to think on her own terms (albeit more by intuition), thus inevitably going against her mother, in all daringness, by breaking all these conventional prescriptions governing femininity on all levels.

Firmly believing the incompatibility between her nature and the nurture, she first cleverly and utterly defies the various disciplining teachers found for her by her mother. For instance, when told by her manners teacher to make a curtsy like a lady, she deliberately shocks her and her fellow students by making farting-like noises. When she returns home, she tricks her mother into believing that she has won her manners teacher's heart-felt approval. For another instance, when she is taught by her piano teacher to practice classical music, she habitually eats from the bowl of plums placed on the piano merely for decoration. Such a behaviour displeases the teacher so much that she tells Annie not to come back again, which is exactly what Annie desires.

Later, she goes even further by directly talking back to her mother on several occasions. The first of its kind occurs after she accidentally sees her mother in bed with her father, with her hand making a circular motion on his back. After being accused by her mother of standing there doing nothing all day, she, with a certain vague feeling of hurt due to her exclusion from her parents' marital bliss, defiantly replies to her mother: "And what if I do?" (31), thus shaming and temporarily silencing her powerful mother, a reversal of their usual pattern.

Later, when she is unfortunately intercepted and forced to talk to a bunch of bullying boys who try to make fun of her, she has no idea that such a scene is witnessed by her mother. Back at home, her enraged mother severely examines her with a frightening look devoid of any love or care, and then goes even further by accusing her of being a slut who makes a shameful spectacle of herself. The damaging effect of such a word on Annie is indeed nothing short of being tremendous: "The word 'slut' (in patois) was repeated over and over, until suddenly I felt as if I were drowning in a well but instead of the well being filled with water it was filled with the word 'slut', and it was pouring in through my eyes, my ears, my nostrils, my mouth." (102) For a second time, Annie feels that she is in terrible need of defending or rescuing herself, thus uttering her most severe and most profound talking-back: "Well...like mother like daughter" (102). This amounts to saying that if Annie is indeed so despicable a slut, it is her mother, not herself, who makes her so. As a critic aptly comments, by "talking back, Annie assumes, temporarily, power over her contemptuous mother."①

Not only showing a defiant gesture to her mother per se at home, Annie also learns to reject Gwen, a proper little girl who can be seen as her mother's variation in school and fully meets with her mother's approval, finding her stereotypedness and silliness increasingly unappetising and unbearable— "a bundle of who said what and who did what" (92). Instead, she befriends, even on highly intimate terms, the unpopular Red Girl, who is arguably Annie's dark double and utterly opposite to her mother in every possible way, fully shown in her

---

① J. Brooks Bouson, *Jamaica Kincaid: Writing Memory, Writing Back to the Mother* (Albany: State University of New York Press, 2005), 50.

dirty dress, red hair that is matted and tangled, fingernails that collect a lot of dirt, and especially her unbelievable and wonderful (to Annie) smell that only someone who has never been forced to bathe and comb herself can possibly have. Their defiant intimacy can be most strikingly seen in the fact that even after Red Girl leaves, she still manages to rescue her and be together with her in her dreams. In the absence of her dark double and her utter rejection of her own mother, she miraculously, and also almost inevitably finds a surrogate mother figure in Ma Chess, her maternal grandmother, who "represents not only family ties but Annie John's (and Jamaica Kincaid's) cultural rituals and roots and traditional consultation with diviners or conjurers"① . By practising Obeah, an Antiguan (not English) ritual, Ma Chess mysteriously rescues Annie from a shame-related illness caused by Annie's mother. After recovering from it, Annie eventually decides to leave both her mother and motherland once and for all, thus commencing the construction of her own, new, and independent self in the future. Against this backdrop, her declaration that "(m)y name is Annie John" (131) indeed sounds especially powerful as a naming, self-defining event in a female Bildungsroman.

Unsettlingly, Annie's apparently (in a way truly so) self-empowering rebellion against and abandonment of her mother ultimately comes at a heavy cost for her. By choosing to utterly hate her mother, she deliberately conceals the other side of the complex, love-hate relationship between mother and daughter— her mother's love for her, as

① Moira Ferguson, *Jamaica Kincaid: Where the Land Meets the Body* (Charlottesville and London: University Press of Virginia, 1994), 69.

well as her own love for her mother. It is undoubtedly an extremely painful experience to attempt to erase it. Just as the 15-year-old melancholy Annie meditates in her private reveries, "Something I could not name just came over us, and suddenly I had never loved anyone or hated anyone so. But to say hate—what did I mean by that? Before, if I hated someone I simply wished the person dead. But I couldn't wish my mother dead. If my mother died, what would become of me? I couldn't imagine my life without her. Worse than that, if my mother died I would have to die, too, and even less than I could imagine my mother dead could I imagine myself dead." (88)

More importantly, the sheer severance of the mother-daughter bond once and for all also inevitably denies Annie a very important part of the past in her life, a memory that still insists on shaping and informing her present and future identities. In other words, the attempt to cut the link with the past is bound to make the present and the future problematic.

In fact, the abandonment of the bond in the past can never be complete or full, for the invisible and inseparable power of the mother (or the mother's shadow) can never leave Annie even after her physical departure from Antigua. What's more, despite her reluctance to admit it, Annie herself has unwittingly internalised the matriarchal disciplining and punishment into her very being by already learning to practice the same shaming mechanism as her mother, such as contempt and affected arrogance. "Like mother like daughter" (102), a remark she used to make during her onetime talking-back to her mother, has ironically become an eternal curse that is bound to remain on her for the rest of her life (or more broadly speaking, all the post-colonial

Caribbean women, no matter if they live in their own country, or elsewhere).

In a sense, the extremely intense, even obsessive concentration on the complex mother-daughter relationship in *Annie John* and other works, or as one critic aptly calls, "the specter of endless autobiography"①, largely contributes to Jamaica Kincaid's huge success in the international literary scene. It is both a bold fictional experimentation and a highly personal, intimate means of catharsis, which Kincaid balances so carefully and so well, a feat that many others do attempt to accomplish, and yet fail terribly.

---

① Leigh Gilmore, *The Limits of Autobiography*: *Trauma and Testimony* (Ithaca: Cornell University Press, 2001), 96.

Chapter 9 Towards a Radical Feminism through the Grotesque Female Body as the Symbolic Site of Power: Reading Kate Grenville's *Lilian's Story* (Australia)

"Stunning...Immensely imagined and original." ——*Observer*

"Grenville's prose is breathtaking and her novel is a miracle of characterisation...This is a rare and beautiful book." ——*Boston Globe*

Now firmly established as one of the most celebrated women writers both in Australia and abroad, Kate Grenville (1950–) has been awarded numerous literary prizes, such as the Australian/Vogel Literary Award, the Commonwealth Writers' Prize, and Britain's Orange Prize. What firmly sets her apart from other fellow women writers, especially in the early stage of her brilliant career, is her unflinchingly, radically and highly recognisably feminist stance on the woman question, as is most fully shown in *Lilian's Story*, a creative re-invention of the Sydney eccentric Bea Miles. By foregrounding the heroine's grotesque female body as the symbolic site of female power, Grenville severely questions and eventually subverts the largely problematic and yet often taken-for-granted authority of the patriarchy, vividly represented by Albion, her authoritarian father.

The Initial Patriarchal Regulation of the Female Child's Body through Corporeal Punishment

In the deeply-entrenched patriarchal woman-hater's mindset, the female body, even a female child's, is often a much-hated site that must be avoided at all costs, or belittled as a nonentity. To prevent it from helping the female shape her own subjectivity with its inevitable growth, the patriarchy feels obliged to constantly discipline and punish this body as it wills.

From the very beginning of the novel, the birth of Lilian the girl in the Singer home at the end of Victorian Australia incites great fury and hatred in the patriarchal Albion Singer, who has expected a male child as his future heir. The only morbid comfort he can find from this birth is the fertility of his wife, who in his hands is increasingly turned into a merely lifeless body whose sole function is to bear him a son.

As the unblessed girl grows up, she constantly feels slighted and-discriminated by her father, especially compared to John, her younger brother. What's more, she starts to receive various rigid instructions from her father on how to train herself to be an obedient, respectable and decent lady in the future, exactly like her own mother. However, her natural curiosity for the unknown and secret world, her fondness for knowledge, and her dislike of self-enclosure contribute to her accidental discovery of her father's closely-guarded secret concerning his unconventional widowed sister, and her naughty and yet pardonable play with a lovely boy of her age in the tree. In the father's eyes, such acts on Lilian's part amount to a severe defiance of everything taught by him, thus deserving equally severe corporeal punishment. For the former "misbehaviour", Lilian receives a harsh spanking on her shamefully revealed bottom from her father's belt; for the latter, she receives a practically deafening slap on her face.

"Fatness" as the Female Child's Radical Survival Strategy

Under the overwhelming oppression and intimidation from patriarchy, an intelligent female child is often faced with two equally unsavoury choices: either to submit to it as an accomplice, thus inevitably being deprived of her self once and for all; or to show a defiant gesture by rebelling against it for the moment, despite the fact that she necessarily invites more severe punishments thereafter. How to be uncooperative and yet unafraid of later retaliations from patriarchy, then, becomes a crucial question for her to ponder over.

For Lilian, her body that serves as the useful site for the father's ideological control and regulation of her femininity becomes the very site of her self-empowerment. By deliberately and consciously "filling" up her small and frail body into a fat and even grotesque one through gluttony, Lilian manages to achieve two goals: to better endure any corporeal punishment from her father; and to deconstruct the father's stereotyped dictates on her being a lady that is destined to be nothing but a wife and a mother, thus "avoiding the inescapably constraining futures that await pretty bourgeois girls"[①]. There is no denying that

① Ruth Barcan, "'Mobility is the Key': Bodies, Boundaries, and Movement in Kate Grenville's *Lilian's Story*," in *Lighting Dark Places: Essays on Kate Grenville*, ed. Sue Kossew (Amsterdam: Rodopi, 2010), 95.

"fatness" as a counter-measure for patriarchal disciplining is indeed morbid. However, in the specific context where the young Lilian is situated, this is practically the only feasible survival strategy for her to adopt.

The Escalation in Patriarchal Control of the Young Woman's Body through Sexual Violation

Despite the patriarchy's frequent inclination to reduce the much-hated and despised female body to a silent nonentity, it also secretly desires it, especially a mature or maturing one, as the potential object for both sexual gratification and display of sexual prowess (a not infrequent sign of masculinity that is arbitrarily constructed by patriarchy). Apparently, these two inclinations seem to be contradictory. However, beneath it lies the same patriarchal urge to govern, regulate, and objectify women as the inferior "other".

As Lilian comes into adulthood, the various increasingly visible signs of maturation on her body (most noticeably her protruding breasts), and her already large figure, combine to make her sexually attractive. With her fast maturation in body, her intelligence in mind also increases quickly, especially after her entrance into university, thus posing even more threats to the law of the father. In fact, more than once, Lilian secretly wishes to "transgress" into his father's study, where he collects all the Dickensian "facts" as writing materials, a symbolic site of patriarchal authority.

In this context, Albion finds it increasingly difficult to regulate her daughter. Such old means as slapping and spanking in Lilian's childhood become increasingly insufficient and ineffective. To defeat this disobedient young woman once and for all, he resorts to one of the most terrible and terrifying means imaginable in any kind of narrative: sexual violation of her own daughter during one dark night, when she is misled into believing him to be already out and freely and triumphantly exploring the (deemed) vacated house.

The act of rape is itself traumatic to any victim. When the perpetrator of this hideous crime is the victim's father, this act inevitably becomes even more unsettling, with far more severe consequences. Both Lilian's panicky voice— "a thin reedy cry like something choking and not being rescued" (154)[①] and her incapacity to tell the truth to anyone else, including her own mother, vividly show the unspeakable damages this terrible event in her life has made to her psyches.

The Spectacle of the Grotesque Female Body in Madness and Mobility as the Young Woman's Subversive Strategy

Arguably, a traumatic event not only has immediate and shocking effects on the traumatised body in the time of its occurrence, but also lingers in his/her memory for a prolonged period. To heal, or at least to alleviate the damages done, a traumatised person tends to adopt various strategies, the most frequent of which is to make all kinds of attempts to forget the traumatising event itself. However, such attempts often fail in the end, not least because of its contingency in

---

① Kate Grenville, *Lilian's Story* (Edinburgh: Canongate, 2007). Subsequent citations to this work are given as parenthetical page references in the text.

nature. Therefore, instead of avoiding it for fear of its reminder of the frail and helpless body in the traumatic past, the traumatised person sometimes chooses to deliberately look the trauma in the face, thus paradoxically reducing the power of the terrifying hold of the traumatic memory through "non-forgetting".

For Lilian, the traumatic experience of being raped by her own father not only shocks her into momentary silence, but also paradoxically strengthens her will to rebel even more firmly. Therefore, for the very first time in her life, she feigns madness, and starts to openly display her traumatised naked body in front of the crowd as a sharp and fierce revenge for her father's bestial act. Undoubtedly, this spectacle greatly enrages her "respectable" father, who condemns Lilian as a shameless bitch.

Not only does she show her naked fat body to the others so as to shame her father, Lilian also habitually escapes from the symbolic house of the father and roams outside, carrying her large body. Just as she remarks, "Mobility is the key." (244)

Despite the sensationalism that is caused by the act itself, Lilian's spectacle of the grotesque female body in madness and mobility does function in positive ways: both showing everyone the powerlessness of the supposedly all-powerful law of the father, and empowering the supposedly powerless, objectified female body, which becomes a key metonymy for the rising female consciousness.

Official Imprisonment of the Defiant Female Body

When private, domestic means alone can no longer contain

women effectively, the patriarchy often resorts to other, more official institutions for more severe means of regulation, among which is the Focauldian madhouse, where the supposedly mad women are thrown and often indeed driven mad due to its poor food, poor housing, irresponsible caring, and various physical violence from other inmates.

This is exactly the case with Lilian, whose increasingly defiant gesture towards Albion forces him to put her into the dehumanising madhouse, where Lilian has to bear the bounding of the authorities, as well as the harassment and bodily injuries done by other women inmates. The only pleasure for her lies in the creative recitation of Shakespeare's lines, with which she can identity herself and enters another world other than the one which imprisons her.

Re-assertion of the Female Bodily Space through Roaming

The bodily confinement and damage imposed by patriarchy on a woman not only traumatises her, but also paradoxically defines for her the real meaning of her body and its potential in shaping her true identity exactly on that basis.

In the novel, the madhouse experience does teach her more than suffering itself. In fact, she truly understands that it is exactly due to her uniqueness (not her wrongness) that fills patriarchy with so much fear that it has to confine her. Therefore, when Aunt Kitty manages to rescue her from the madhouse, she embarks on a life truly of her own. The fat, large body that is much despised, reviled, and damaged by patriarchy begins to assume a truly positive, constructive meaning for Lilian herself (no longer a radical, subversive strategy alone), who in turn tries to drive this meaning home to others she meets when freely roaming around the city. For instance, she constantly hops on and off all possible public transports, such as buses, ferries, hijacks taxis, and finally is chauffeured around her city for one last tour. During the rides, she never fails to impress the various drivers with her unusual and yet confident, space-filling body, and her masterly Shakespeare recitations. Gradually, she even turns herself into a public celebrity whose stories are taken home by the drivers, and retold time and again generation after generation. In other words, she truly makes "her-story" in her own way, a different, and yet equally, if not more authentic and meaningful history than "History".

From the initial patriarchal objectification of the female body through corporeal punishment and sexual violation, to the enlightened female assertion of her grotesque body as a symbolic site of power in constructing an independent, meaningful female identity that is no less powerful than males in its influences, Lilian does make considerable progress as a radical feminist. This is why Kate Grenville's novel and its film adaptation still resonate in the minds of today's readers for their unique inspirations and warnings.

Chapter 10 The Power of Voyeurism and Its Limits: Reading Janet Frame's "The Linesman" (New Zealand)

"Frame is, and will remain, divine." ——Alice Sebold

"A poetic soul has rarely come better disguised." ——Jane Campion

Acclaimed as one of New Zealand's greatest writers, Janet Frame (1924 – 2004) has garnered numerous awards and prizes both in her native country and abroad for her oeuvre, such as New Zealand Book Award for Fiction and Commonwealth Writers Prize for Best Book. With a distinctive style that can be roughly defined as modernism, magic realism, and postmodernism, she manages to chart a variety of complex and ambiguous human psyches in unprecedented ways. Among her fiction, "The Linesman", a mere-two-page-length short story from *The Reservoir: Stories and Sketches*, tellingly shows her precision and deftness in exploring the power of voyeurism and its limits.

From the very start, the unnamed first-person narrator, very possibly a female writer just like Janet Frame herself①, seems to be merely depicting, with a marked nonchalance, a very commonly observed

① This connection between the narrator and the author is largely warranted by the highly autobiographical nature of almost all Frame's works.

scene and a few equally commonly seen people. However, as the story unfolds, many hidden parallels are increasingly revealed here, namely the parallel between writing and repair work, as well as the parallel between the writer and the linesman.

Arguably, the former parallel can be seen in the following ways. First, both writing and repair work are complicated, demanding work. Just as a linesman has to train himself to be capable of "working, twisting, arranging wires, screwing, unscrewing" (169)①, a writer is also required to constantly design, redesign, construct, reconstruct, and even destroy her various drafts before her final work can be done. Second, both writing and repair work need something to cling to as their refuge. Just as a linesman needs to be "dependent on his safety belt, trusting in it" (169), a writer also necessarily depends on a certain belief in her inner genius before writing anything at all. Third, both writing and repair work necessarily result in a sense of precarious balance. Just like a linesman "seeming in a position of comfort and security" (169), a writer also constantly oscillates between belief and doubt about his/her writings.

Besides, the writer and the linesman share an even more unsettling similarity, serving useful "doubles" or "shadows" for each other: both are placed in a "spying" position, thus being capable of "legitimately" observing the private world within a house. This is undoubtedly a special power bestowed on a commonly assumed non-pow-

---

① Janet Frame, *The Daylight and the Dust*: *Selected Short Stories* (London: Virago Press, 2010). Subsequent citations to this work are given as parenthetical page references in the text.

erful subject, be it the writer or a linesman. Paradoxically, this visual power seemingly acquired by the non-powerful subject exactly shows his or her "powerlessness" —when the subject under the voyeuristic gaze finally separates himself from the voyeur by various means (such as drawing the curtains), both the writer and the linesman are forced to ponder over such despairing absences in disillusion and despair. When intensified, these feelings can be translated into self-destructive impulses. When the first person narrator "was hoping that he might fall" (170), she is very probably harbouring the same urges for herself.

On a more profound level, the visual power imposed on readers or dwellers by both the writer and the linesman reflect a morbid desire for communication and connection between different men in an increasingly alienating and alienated contemporary society. Since ordinary or normal ways of communication, such as verbal language and body language, have become increasingly difficult and even practically impossible, suspicions and grudges necessarily rise up between men. Ironically, the only means left for men to realise such a desire for connection is necessarily abnormal, such as voyeurism and spying. To some extent, such morbid behaviours can indeed induce, at least contingently, an orgasmic satisfaction in voyeurs. However, just because the social factors that contribute to, or heighten the occurrence of such behaviours are inherently problematic, these behaviours are doomed to fail at length—neither the writer nor the linesman can derive true, lasting happiness from their respective acts.

Chapter 11 From "We" to "I": A Samoan Girl's Self-awakening in Sia Figiel's *Where We Once Belonged* (Samoa)

"Sia Figiel is a major literary voice ushering the vastness of Pacific Rim literatures into the millennium." ——Lois-Ann Yamanaka

"Sia Figiel has written a passion, a song of longing and loss, a song of fire." ——Junot Diaz

Apart from Australia and New Zealand, other Oceanic countries are largely ignored by international communities for their apparent obscurity and insignificance in literary production. However, in recent years, this unfair silence has been gradually broken, for a new host of writers from these less developed Oceanic countries have given unforgettable voice to both their countries and their womanhood, most notably Sia Figiel (1967 –) from Samoa. So far, she has penned two highly acclaimed novels, including *Where We Once Belonged*, which was duly awarded the 1997 Commonwealth Writers' Prize for fiction, South East Asia/South Pacific region.

In *Where We Once Belonged*, Figiel manages to weave a complex and yet highly accessible tale of Samoan puberty blues, in a writing style emblematic of *Su'ife-filoi*, a Samoan form of story telling centered around the "quilt-like weaving of words"① . Arguably, the main

① Jacinta Galea'i, *A Novel in Prose and Poetry*, Ph. D. dissertation, University of Hawaii, May 2005.

heroine named Alofa (meaning "love" in the Samoan language) goes through several uneasy stages in her eventful development as a girl in the village of Malaefou, Samoa.

The Uneasy Relationship Between Mother and Daughter

In contemporary Samoan life, the unequal treatment of men (boys) and women (girls) is still very rampant and pervasive. A pregnant Samoan woman often bears a highly ambivalent attitude towards her conception: both joy (for motherhood) and fear (for the possibility of bearing a female child). If the relationship between the woman and the man who impregnates her remains a precarious one (for instance, the woman is a mere mistress, not a wife), the fear is bound to outweigh the joy. Therefore, the birth of a daughter is almost inevitably seen as a disaster by the woman, thus spelling doom for any healthy or sound relationship between a mother and a daughter in the future.

In the novel, Pisa, Alofa's mother, suffers from such a dilemma. Young, intelligent and promising, she is duly expected to get a scholarship and go to New Zealand for study. However, she is unfortunately seduced by a middle-aged man who is actually a nobody and has married two wives (the first committing suicide). The seduction ends in her carrying a child of his within her womb. The merely 18-year-old (a child herself) Pisa is thrown into an abyss of anxieties and uncertainties. The only possibility for her to change her fate is to bear a male child for him. In that way, she may have some say in renegotiating the tripartite relationship.

However, even from her conception of Alofa, Pisa has a sense of doom that she may carry a girl child. As Alofa later recounts, even she, the to-be-born baby, has willed herself as a girl (quite against her mother's wish). When she finally gives birth to Alofa, she feels devastated. It is now her belief that she, just like her equally ill-fated mother, has fallen into a vicious cycle in which one generation after another is seduced and impregnated by bad men, only to bear girls who are raised to be seduced by more bad men when they grow up. That's why she cannot help hating Alofa, her own daughter, like a disease and believing her to have killed her son. She refuses to look at her, feed her with her own milk, or name her. She deliberately makes Alofa's look ugly, dresses her in an ugly manner, and makes her feel ugly. In a word, she does every possible thing (except child-killing) to humiliate, hurt or damage her, just as she is herself damaged by those hostile villagers' words, gestures and eyes during her pregnancy.

As Alofa grows up, she becomes an increasingly sensitive and inquisitive spirit, ambitiously and eagerly comparing with her female friends in every possible way (such as the arrival of moon sickness, the size of the breast, among other things), as well as comparing with boys (such as mathematics). Thus, she cannot allow her own mother to slight or mistreat her for the mere reason that she is born a girl, just like the rebellious baby she used to be in Pisa's womb. She cannot fathom why her mother attaches such importance to men (instead of her own achievement). She tells herself that she will never look at them. For her, men do not exist. Far from meaning that she hates men, this internal declaration nevertheless shows clearly that Alofa refuses to be traumatised, victimised, or self-victimised in a largely patriarchal society with which even women collude. She wants to be optimistic, to be UNLIKE Pisa, Pisa's mother or any other self-pitying woman. She is eager to prove that being a girl is a thing to take pride in, not a thing to be sad or pessimistic about.

In a sense, the uneasy relationship between Pisa and Alofa forces the latter to encounter the difficulties of being a woman. More importantly, this struggle teaches Alofa to reevaluate the value of being a modern Samoan woman that can and should break the stereotyped fate which is taught and self-practiced by those older, more traditional women.

The Complex Lesson from the Village Fool

For contemporary Samoans, New Zealand, Australia, Europe and America offers something quite different from their own native land (at least in their imagination). Therefore, more and more Samoans try all means to go abroad for self-discovery, including some Samoan women. Ironically, the western education is sometimes instrumental in teaching the Samoans the very meaning of being a true Samoan who should get away from too much western influence and keep their old traditions, customs, practices and languages intact. Thus, upon their return to Samoa, their new, independent ways of thinking may be misunderstood by their compatriots, thus being labelled as fools or maniacs.

In the novel, it is Siniva, the sister of Alofa's father who makes a shocking self-discovery after studying abroad. It dawns upon her that church-going, behaving, thinking, or speaking in a western way only kills themselves as Samoans. Therefore, she is eager to tell the white people in Samoa that Gauguin is dead, and also eager to tell her Samoan compatriots that Jesus Christ is not a Samoan. However, she is almost misunderstood by all, especially her family members who brutally beat her up again and again. They even try to exorcise her, believing that a ghost has invaded her. When all attempts to "help" her fail, she is eternally marginalised, exiled by all, who are either sad for or angry with her (no third alternative in feeling). She becomes the (in) famous "village fool" who lives separately and secretly in a God-forsaken house.

For Alofa, the outsider status enjoyed by Siniva is certainly a bad thing, a thing to be avoided (as we know, Alofa is eager to make friends). However, paradoxically, this status also seems enviable in a strange way, for it offers a new way of thinking, an "individual" way, a way of "I", not the suffocating "we". In a restless and adventurous age when she feels more than suffocated by the moralistic and meaningless teachings of teachers, pastors and parents, Siniva is more like a daring spirit, refreshing and sharpening her mind and soul. That's why Siniva's suicide at the end of the novel is interpreted by Alofa neither as a failure nor as an easily forgotten triviality. In a world that refuses to show leniency or understanding to an intelligent woman in the disguise of a fool, the only way for her is to leave it behind once and for all. In fact, Alofa also develops her own way of "dying" in sleep in order to get away from the control from the dominant others. Unlike Siniva, however, she knows that this unjust earthly world still needs a living (not dead) woman warrior to redress its wrongs, and she is willing to shoulder that sacred responsibility or mission all alone without fear or anxiety. That's why she begins "walking-walking...away from Siniva's grave...walking now towards Malaefou, towards the new gathering place where 'we' once belonged." (239)①

To some extent, the presence of Siniva offers Alofa both a new path and a dead end. Fortunately, Alofa indeed learns an important lesson from Siniva, namely learning to be "I". At the same time, she does not simply abandon the world for honouring her own ideals. Instead, she daringly chooses to live in this harsh world, deciding to fight until the very end for her independence as a modern girl and woman. In more than one way, it is truly a great choice.

Self-Awakening through the Ritual of Sex

For a girl who seeks to know herself, role models (or their opposites) are indeed of great necessity as possible references (or warnings). However, they are far from being sufficient. A girl still needs to bump and struggle for her own unique way of life, with her (and other people's) bodies often serving as a crucial site for this struggle.

As can be seen, in the novel, besides the various (and largely conflicting) influences from Pisa and Siniva, Alofa also gets greatly influenced by her sight of, or contact with various bodies, both female and male.

At the very beginning of the novel, Alofa's first sight of the insides of a woman's vagina instills in her the sense that she is biologi-

① Sia Figiel, Where We Once Belonged (New York: Kaya Press, 1999).

cally a woman (not a man). She cannot help comparing her own body (less developed in so many ways) with this mature female body. However, only after she accidentally witnesses her own father's naked body all too clearly, does she truly and unmistakably realise the biological difference between a man and a woman. Although she feels embarrassed and confused by the fact that her father is not having sex with her mother, but her teacher, she still feels an untold thrill within herself.

For Alofa, the thrill soon gives way to fear and puzzlement, for the various stories of her young female neighbours and friends who get pregnant and have to be sent away strikes her greatly. She suddenly becomes uneasy with her maturing process. What's more, the punished party is always the girl, not the boy (who is always easily forgiven and remains at large). She vaguely senses the obvious imbalance in the power structure of sexes.

However, Alofa still refuses to be discouraged, and continues her self-discovery without hesitation. Since she is fond of Lealofi, the pastor's son who is good at playing the piano, she cannot help touching him, especially after his encouragement. For the first time, she experiences the real sensation of holding a penis in her own hand. When they are caught, Alofa is severely punished by her father (he himself used to be caught in adultery with her teacher, but he can remain unpunished and unapologetic to anyone), who uses all possible means to shame her, such as slapping her face and shaving her head time and again. For Alofa, the reason why her father shames her so much is that she DARES to be LIKE him. She, a mere girl, DARES to commit the same transgressive act LIKE him. This is utterly outrageous for him.

Arguably, this village scandal exerts a great impact on Alofa's personal development by showing her the very hypocrisy of a western-leaning Samoan patriarchal disciplinarian. She knows she is powerless to fight, but she at least gets the true knowledge of what the world is, unlike many girls who still remain in darkness, as her aunt Siniva rightfully believes. She secretly hopes that in her adulthood (which will soon come in due time), a stronger "she" will not only change her own fate, but also blaze the trail for other fellow Samoan women.

Throughout the novel, Figiel's vivid and authentic portrayal of Alofa, be it in her interactions with other women that mean much to her, or in her sexual awakening, does provide the readers, especially those who often have a condescending attitude towards Oceanic authors, with a clear counter-statement: both the Samoan nation and womanhood are unyielding in their independent stance, and they refuse to live in darkness and ignorance any longer.

Chapter 12 Female Resilience and Subtle Defiance against Ideological Policing: Reading Yiyun Li's "Souvenir" (United States/China)

"Brilliant...a frighteningly lucid vision of human fate."

——*Publishers Weekly* (Starred Review)

"In the most dismal circumstances and with the most unlikely subjects, Yiyun Li has the rare ability to conjure hope. She writes with precision and delicacy about the Chinese diaspora and about the new China, and in doing so she writes about us all."

——Mona Simpson

Although now being American by citizenship, Beijing-born Yiyun Li (1972–), acclaimed Frank O'Connor International Short Story Award winner, is still as much of a Chinese as she can be. The subject matter that she mostly touches upon, the way she tells her tales, and the philosophy of life that informs her characters, are invariably of a Chinese nature. What especially merits noticing is her often complex and yet highly convincing portrayal of various Chinese women in the new China, as is probably most eloquently seen in "Souvenir" from *Gold Boy, Emerald Girl*, her latest collection of short stories.

In this short story that covers mere six pages, much of the drama unfolds only psychologically, with sparing dialogues almost at the end. However, through the lens of double narration from an unnamed old man and an unnamed young girl, the unprecedented resilience and subtle defiance of a modern, liberated heroine against severe ideological policing gradually surfaces.

Ideological Policing from State Apparatuses, Workplaces and Civil Society

Instead of directly dealing with a political subject or event, Yiyun Li deftly allows the old man and the young girl, her two protagonists, to reveal, in a natural and non-deliberate way, their own life stories in their observation of and meditations on other people's life.

The revelation that scatters here and there in the story is indeed startling, bringing to light a nation state that is largely policed by dominant ideologies that are capable of repressing, oppressing and punishing any dissenting voices that dare to challenge or question the law of the FATHER. Specifically, such policing is achieved in both ways.

Explicitly, state apparatuses like the police, courts, and prisons arrest, sentence and then imprison these dissenters, thus forcing them to obey the authority in power. As the girl narrates, she has seen enough of her fellowmen's protests, bloodshed, arrests and interrogations in the past two years. Even the boy hero that she has fallen for is crushed by the severe interrogations and officially announced as a madman who is deprived of the ability to marry her any more.

Implicitly, various workplaces, or "units (dan wei)", also appropriate the means of ideological control from the state apparatuses for their own uses. The clear-cut hierarchical power structure in these places almost inevitably coerces, although in a subtle and non-forceful way, anyone inferior in the social ladder to obey the superior's every command, and to compete, often in a malicious way, with each other for a higher position and more recognition from the superior. As the old man narrates, her now deceased wife used to be taken advantage of by her colleagues who tried desperately to get promotions that belonged to her. As the girl narrates, she herself, among many other girls, used to be sexually harassed by her physics professor, who dared to believe that his superior status in college confers on him a power to do anything on his mind, including making preys of his female students.

A larger, more terrifying pattern of ideological control permeates the society as a whole, especially in people's daily lives. As the man observes, the girl moves very cautiously, even vigilantly, "as if she was aware that anyone, anything, could run her over without the slightest idea of her existence" (198 – 199)① . This shows the almost existential fear hidden in people's hearts, largely caused by the dehumanising, all-pervasive ideological control that ignores and even denies individuals' right to live as decent human beings. This reminds the man of his own wife, who used to be equally fearful of the larger society, for she was also taken advantage of by many unfriendly strangers cutting into the lines in front of her. Even the man's open, unashamed intrusion into the girl's personal life is also influenced by this highly infectious desire to control others.

---

① Yiyun Li, *Gold Boy*, *Emerald Girl* (New York: Random House, 2010). Subsequent citations to this work are given as parenthetical page references in the text.

Subtle Ideological Control of Femininity

Besides silencing any potentially subversive men in various ways including force, the dominant ideology also needs to exert its patriarchal control on women and girls, although mostly in a subtle manner. The subtlety mainly lies in the deliberate cultivation and eulogizing of an ideal femininity that features obedience and innocence, utterly devoid of any trace of sexuality. When women and girls refuse to be pigeonholed into such a reductive and repressive category, they tend to be ridiculed, slandered, accused, and even punished.

From the beginning, the unnamed young girl in the story is subjected to the gaze of the apparently patriarchal old① man, who makes silent, irrefutable (in his own mind) judgments of everything about her in his own way. According to him, this girl seems to be indeed innocent and pure, as can be shown by her white dress and her unsexy figure. He even fantasies the girl to be the younger version of his now deceased wife. However, in this context, such innocence really means ignorance, or easy prey to patriarchal control.

The open and direct confrontation between the two parties occurs when the patriarchal old man comes to the girl and requests her, who

① Despite the wide spread of western values in China, for most Chinese people who are still cultivated or influenced by the traditional Chinese ethics, seniority means wisdom accumulated over a lifetime, thus deserving respectability. However, this overly importance attached to seniority sometimes makes old people consciously or unconsciously self-satisfied, believing themselves to be right in all things. Therefore, in a way, old people, especially old men unwittingly become the most die-hard patriarchs.

hardly knows him yet, to drink chrysanthemum tea with him. In fact, this strange request is more like an order that is less than friendly.

Having her own troubles in mind, the girl feels quite helpless with his unexpected request. Escaping into the pharmacy, she finds herself still followed by him, who tenaciously offers her another request for a bowl of wonton soup. After being quietly rejected by the girl, he finally shows his vehemence, for he simply cannot stand a girl who looks like his own wife to treat him so indifferently.

It is worth mentioning that the old man's die-hard obsession with his various unreasonable patriarchal demands seems to be closely related to his widower status. No longer having a wife, a rightful and exclusive property under his name to exert his power (possibly in the name of love) over, he needs to find replacement in others. That's why he has followed many other young girls and women besides the female protagonist. The only difference is, this time, he means it more than any other time.

What further infuriates and unsettles the old man is the girl's open—albeit with a marked sense of shyness and shame that indeed befits her innocence—purchase of the pink pack of condoms in the pharmacy. This amounts to being a decisive subversion of his self-constructed fantasy of what a good girl should be like. He does not really care to know the true reason for the girl's "shameless" act, for the act itself already deserves a severe condemnation, or at least a severe warning on his part.

Buoyed by his self-claiming high moral ground, he does offer his warning to the girl, taking it for granted that the girl will listen to him this time. However, the girl refutes his persuasion again, forcing him to be aware of the difference between his submissive wife and this stubborn girl. To safeguard his moral and ideological correctness, he accepts his overestimation of the girl, judging her to be much inferior to his own wife.

What's worse, many women internalise the patriarchal ideology governing womanhood, and even take pride or delight in their complicity in its control of their own sex. The most eloquent and telling example is offered by the two middle-aged saleswomen in the pharmacy, with one sitting behind the cash register and the other behind the counter. Their endless, highly-charged exchange of information concerning their husbands not only shows their ennui and boredom with their own uncreative jobs, but also point to their very dependence on men: without them as subject matters for chats, they will find their own life as women basically meaningless. The only interest they can find in fellow women comes from their equally, if not more, sharp-tongued condemnation or accusation of weaker, less powerful women or girls in order to please men and win their approval, both in the presence and absence of actual men. As a consequence, they show unfriendly uncooperativeness when the girl wants to buy the condoms, utterly showing disrespect for her status as a customer. Not only do they deliberately force the girl to say outright that she wants to buy "condoms" instead of "those" as a euphemism, they also contemptuously laugh at such a purchase, secretly believing her to be a slut or an indecent girl. The last and most humiliating insult they make of the girl is to throw her the pack of condoms, which cannot help falling on the floor. The small pharmacy, in such a context, becomes an ugly site of verbal and psychological damage cruelly done to women by women in the name of morality and ideological correctness.

Female Resilience and Subtle Defiance against Patriarchy

Despite her unfriendly surroundings that show signs of overwhelming ideological control almost everywhere she goes, and also despite her young age, the girl displays a rare strength and resilience that far exceeds her own age. From the very start, she clearly knows her powerlessness as a female and a common citizen. Unfazed by it, however, she learns to well protect herself against any threatening or harmful forces. That's why she is always cautious and vigilant.

Besides successfully protecting herself, the girl also shows her subtle defiance against the equally subtle patriarchal ideological control by showing her Madonna-like capacity for love and encouragement of the boy hero who has suffered from dehumanising interrogations and is now officially announced to be a madman. The act of purchasing condoms does not mean that she takes liberty with her body. Instead, it highlights her unquenchable will to save a once heroic man, as well as her unshakable belief in his eventual recovery through the consoling agency of her loving body, which is all the more moving when the extremely difficult circumstances for their love are taken into account.

Besides self-protection and salvation of loved ones, the girl also shows a rare and hardly imitable ability to be sympathetic and forgiving for those who bully, accuse, or hurt her in various ways. Throughout the entire interaction with both the old man and the two middle-aged women, she does not, even for once, said or done anything that is directly retaliatory or revengeful, such as talking back to them, cursing them, or ridiculing them. As the girl herself aptly thinks to herself, "she was not that person" (203). What she most cares about is not simply to get even for a sense of morbid and short-lived satisfaction in a society that engenders and even perversely encourages mutual hatred or hurt among its citizens (more like subjects of a kingdom or monarchy), who constantly oscillate between the position of being a victim and that of being a victimiser. Instead, what she really cares about is to bring back long lost or forgotten hope and human faith in life to all these traumatised and traumatising people, including her beloved boyfriend, the two middle-aged women, and the old man. Despite the fact that the two women and the old man still cling to their state-sanctioned ideologies and values at the end of the story, the shining, graceful presence of this Madonna-like young girl certainly leaves no conscientious reader untouched or unchanged. It is also worth noting that the girl herself also has an optimistic vision of the future when she, as an old lady, will show her children this pink pack of condoms, not as something that brings shame or guilt, but as a highly treasured souvenir, a reminder to them all of her hopeful youth and vitality in spite of the demands of the trying times, as well as of her strong and honest passion for her beloved one when he is most in need of her salvation.

As can be seen here and elsewhere, most of the heroines in Yiyun Li's fiction, including this unnamed (yet paradoxically universal) girl, are often thrown into a hostile context that is highly charged with politics and ideologies. For them, the classic question of "to be or not to be" tends to be both an abstract, profound question for existential queries or meditations, and a down-to-earth question of survival. Paradoxically, the more oppressive and repressive the various ideological controls are, the more resilient these heroines will become. They not only learn to protect themselves against harm, but also learn to bring salvation and hope to their loved ones as well as those who bully, hurt, or accuse them in various ways, thus making them truly Madonna-like, and subtly challenging, deconstructing, subverting the very patriarchal values and ideologies that explicitly and implicitly sanction the dehumanising control of the people, especially women and girls. This is probably also where the biggest strength of Yiyun Li's narrative art lies.

Chapter 13 Beyond the Shadows of the Abuse as a Family Ritual: Reading Shashi Deshpande's *The Dark Holds No Terrors* (India)

"Leaves the reader gasping for breath." ——*Sunday Standard*

"An extremely talented storyteller with an uncommon way with words." ——*Hindustan Times*

In the contemporary Indian literary scene, a host of women novelists in English, such as Arundhati Roy, Shashi Deshapande, Anita Desai, and Kiran Desai, have made an increasingly striking presence, constantly challenging critics and common readers' horizon of expectations. Among them, Sahitya Akademi Award·winning Shashi Deshpande (1938–) still stands apart with a unique voice of her own. Compared with the other three, she may be less internationally known. However, in more than one way, she shows even more insight into the contemporary Indian women's plight, which is most vividly shown in her debut *The Dark Holds No Terrors*. Through the portrayal of a woman's heartrending and yet persistent struggles to escape the shadows of the abuse as a family ritual, Deshpande creatively offers a new way of thinking for women seeking to govern their own fate.

Women's Power over Women: the Strained Relationship between Mother and Daughter

In Indian society, one of the most controversial customs is the bride's dowry, which means that at the time of a woman's marriage, her family has to offer a (often) large sum of money to the groom's family. The implication is all too obvious: a girl is born as a misfortune and a burden to the family, and brought up only to be gotten rid of.

Ironically, more often than not, in many Indian families, the one who most hates the birth of a girl is not the patriarch, but the matriarch. Hardly realising the fact that she also used to be a girl and a bride who suffered the same slight and mistreatment, the matriarch often chooses to compensate for her own suffering by imposing it on her own daughters. At the same time, she tends to indulge the sons' every whim, never believing that they can do anything wrong in any way.

This is exactly the case with Sarita, the heroine in *The Dark Holds No Terrors*. From the very beginning of her life, she acutely observes and feels the sharp differences in her mother's treatment of her and Dhruva, her younger brother. She is told to expect little from life from early on, while Dhruva is always, endlessly treasured, with all the family members' hope on him. That's why her mother feels great dissatisfaction and even rage when Sarita expresses her hope that she can be allowed to go to a medical college in Bombay and financially supported. In her mother's eyes, going to college is of no use for a girl, and it is a sheer waste of money. The money she has to pay for her future marriage is already a big nuisance on her mind, making other expenses or costs for her personal development almost outrageous.

The conflict between Sarita' s mother and Sarita escalates when her brother accidentally gets drowned. In her mother' s view, it is Sarita who kills Dhruva; it is Sarita who insists on taking her brother to the site of danger; it is Sarita who pays little attention to the danger lurking there. If someone has to die, that one should be Sarita, not her dear Dhruva.

The mother' s relentless grudge and hatred for her bring unfathomable traumas to Sarita. The alienation between her and her own home becomes even more intense. Even after her mother' s death, she still clearly feels the hatred of her ghost, who haunts her time and again, never letting her go. Unbearable and endless guilt is fiercely forced on her, despite the fact that she does nothing wrong. In fact, it is Dhruva who compels her to take him to the site of danger, utterly ignoring her warning. Once there, neither Dhruva nor Sarita can reasonably judge the depth of the puddle that will eventually claim Dhruva' s life. Normally, a puddle is indeed by no means so fatal. However, the workers have dug it deep enough, without posting any signs of its danger, thus bringing about the calamity.

As can be seen above, from the initial belittling of her own daughter, to the utterly unreasonable hatred for her, Sarita' s mother typifies the perverted side of womanhood that is complicit with patriarchy. Instead of learning to understand, appreciate and help other women, these once-beleaguered women only learn the importance of poisonous power, which is used to abuse and hurt other women who are in an inferior position. Only by this means, can they get a sense of pleasure and delight, however perverted they may be.

A New Cage and Prison: the Problematic Relationship between Husband and Wife

In contemporary Indian society, a woman not only has to address the often strained relationship between her and her mother, but also has to tackle the even more problematic and tricky relationship between her and her husband. For the latter, her role is at best a subsidiary one. She is expected to be a docile, selfless model wife and mother of many children. She is by no means encouraged to pursue a career of her own. If She does attempt to pursue it, the best response to be expected from a husband is often mere tolerance or endurance. If she even achieves a triumph that overshadows the achievement of her husband, she is bound to be slighted, hated, found fault with by him. For the woman who truly tries hard to balance the various demands from both home and work, her husband's treatment often throws her into a dilemma that is hard to get out of. This new home, more often than not, becomes a new cage and prison.

This is again the case with Sarita. As a girl traumatised by her demanding and uncaring mother, she conceals a secret wish in her heart that she can leave her own home for a better one, and she truly expects someone to cherish, love and care for her. Fortunately (at least for that moment), she encounters the charismatic young poet Manohar, who showers her with loving words and loving gestures. Suddenly, she finds herself not to be the unwanted, unlovable child any more. She regains confidence in her very being. She even becomes a physically aroused woman, re-loving her body that is often said to be ugly and undesirable. In having sex with Mahohar, she feels whole again as a true woman. In a word, she finds redemption in love.

This love does end in a marriage between Sarita and Mahohar. However, unexpectedly (for Sarita), this becomes another beginning of her tragic life: romance soon gives way to sheer, cruel reality. To her surprise, Sarita finds that despite his poetic talent, Mahohar is indeed no different from other men in outlook concerning the relationship between men and women. Like others, he expects her to be the traditional housewife, not a professional. When he finds out that her job as a doctor earns her more money, more respect and more praises than him, he finds it less and less endurable, for he feels his manly pride greatly damaged. Therefore, he not only abuses Sarita in words, but also resorts to domestic rape, showing a truly frightening "dichotomy of her husband's character"① . Now, the sex that used to redeem Sarita in her darkest moments becomes a nightmare for her. She can do nothing but escape the new home again, without knowing the direction to her next destination.

As can be seen above, from the initial redemption of her to the eventual victimisation, the husband plays a truly ambivalent role in Sarita's life, who is forced to reorient her own relationship with him again and again. Fortunately, she still dares to put an end to the status quo instead of being eternally trapped in a helpless way. Although she still has doubts concerning her own future as an independent woman, she still manages to take the first, and the most difficult step, which is

① Mallika A. Nair, "'A Room of One's Own': The Metaphorical Implications of 'House' in Shashi Deshpande's Novels," *Indian Literature*, 54, no. 4 (2010), 178.

still laudable in every possible way.

Be it the relentlessly unapologetic mother, or the sexually abusive husband, the heroine in Shashi Deshpande's *The Dark Holds No Terrors* does go through a lot. It is the tragic reality of not a few contemporary Indian women. However, apart from the various "terrors", Deshpande also shows the readers the optimistic message that "the dark holds no terrors", for the heroine finally realises in the end that she should abandon the various shadows cast on her. She should no longer suffer, or feel shame and guilt for being a "bad" (in other people's eyes) sister, daughter and wife. She learns to refuse the various labels imposed on her, and starts to refashion herself as a new person with a new self, despite the difficulties involved and the uncertainties ahead of her. This may be the most important feminist message Deshpande hopes to convey, indeed with much success.

Chapter 14　Subverting the Stereotyped Plot: Reading Bapsi Sidhwa' s *The Pakistani Bride* (Pakistan)

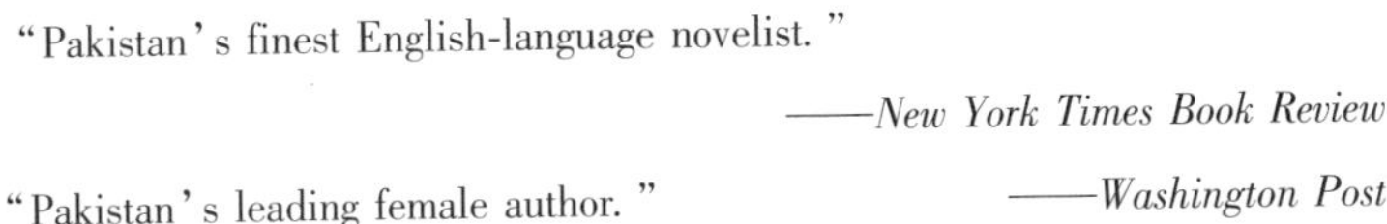

"Pakistan' s finest English-language novelist."

——*New York Times Book Review*

"Pakistan' s leading female author."　——*Washington Post*

Born in Karachi and raised in Lahore, Pakistan, Bapsi Sidhwa (1938-) has garnered a host of national and international accolades for her series of controversial novels that often touch and even break the numerous taboos in the Indian subcontinent. Arguably as her first completed novel (though not her first published one), *The Pakistani Bride* dares to delve into the largely sanctioned domestic violence (even murder) in marriage, one of the most problematic customs or behavioural codes that dominate Pakistan, especially its mountainous backwaters.

As Anita Desai states in her eloquent introduction to *The Pakistani Bride*, this book is based on a true story heard of by its author. This, however, should not mislead us into believing that this book is merely an enlarged version of a news report. In fact, as the story goes on, the narrative morphs into a complex site that is filled with multiple voices that constantly inspire, urge, and even demand us to revise the stereotyped, largely taken-for-granted plot of forced marriage and eventual sacrifice.

From Patriarchal Father to Humanistic "Abba"

The novel's first visible divergence from the conventional plot adopted by many other writers lies in the unusual portrayal of Qasim, the bride Zaitoon's adoptive father. Instead of being reduced to being a mere puppet figure (the merchant who sells his daughter, thus initiating the conventional narrative), Qasim assumes several authentic, highly believable identities of his own in the novel: a reluctant young groom, a loving father and husband, a bereaved widower (losing all his family members one by one), a helpless refugee in the Partition Era. In other words, in the novel, Sidhwa attempts to seek out the human (not simply animalistic) side of the "daughter-selling merchant", implying that Qasim adopts this girl not for potential financial transactions, but for filling the emotional void left by his bereavement.

What's more, Sidhwa goes on to investigate Qasim's necessarily complicated motives during and before his final decision-making. Although it appears that the weightiest reason for his marrying his daughter is his fulfillment of tribal honour, he does show signs of love for his adopted daughter and truly cares about her future happiness. That's why he has a sudden, rarely-found-in-others impulse to cancel his "honoured-above-life-itself" promise just on the verge of Zaitoon's departure.

From Binary Oppositions to Literary Doubles

The novel's second significant breakthrough lies in the shift from mere binary oppositions to literary doubles. As is clearly seen in the novel, the emphasis is no longer placed on the mere difference between the urban plains and the mountainous hinterland in causing Zaitoon's plight. Instead, obviously, Sidhwa pays more attention to the possible ways and strategies available to Zaitoon for her final escape. That's why she aptly introduces Carol, the American bride to a Pakistani Major and arguably Zaitoon's literary double in the novel. Despite their non-acquaintance with each other, Carol, the American bride indeed bears a great resemblance to the bride from Lahore in their initial shared romantic fantasies of the "exotic" and later "shared suffering" in a hostile men's world. What's more, Carol's timely outburst is subtly and yet unmistakably instrumental in changing the Major's attitude towards her and eventually all women, including the runaway bride. In fact, it is the Major who finally rescues the barely living Zaitoon and forces Sakhi, in his great reluctance, to believe in her death and renounce his further man-hunt for Zaitoon.

From Passive Domestic "Bodies" to Resilient "Wills" in Extreme Circumstances

The novel's third breakthrough lies in the successful portrayal of the changes in Zaitoon's personal development. As a girl who is unexpectedly sent to the unfriendly mountainous hinterland with no one to help her out, she first responds to it in a quite passive manner, namely endurance of her husband's always quick temper and rage at anything, no matter how trivial it is; endurance of his severe and endless beating; endurance of his rape-like sex; endurance of his demand for children; endurance of his demand that she should not see any other man besides her husband. In other words, subjected to her husband's all-powerful, disciplining gaze, she becomes an accomplice and merely a living corpse that is deprived of any personal wills, thoughts and feelings.

However, as her own self-consciousness gradually and inevitably rises, she learns to abandon this endless and hopeless complicit behaviour by choosing to escape from this forbidden ground, no matter how risky it can be. As is vividly narrated in the novel, during the escape, she goes through a lot, such as extreme shortage of food and water, extremely harsh weather, labyrinthine mountains that defy anyone's mounting, ever-hungry vultures, rapists, and even more dangerous, tireless tribal men-hunters who are bent on stoning her to a horrible death. However, with her inner and physical strength, Zaitoon manages to weather all, instead of blindly falling victim to her fate, namely being beheaded like the tribal girl startlingly seen by Carol and the Major, or like the tribal girl in the startling news report that inspires Sidhwa's writing of this novel. In a way, through the brand new portrait of the heroine, Sidhwa indeed heralds the arrival of Pakistani feminism in its utterly inspiring form.

Be it in the more realistic portrait of a sophisticated father struggling between his urban present and tribal past, the successful literary doubles used to highlight the universal plight of women, or the modern women's exhilarating change in their daring gestures to challenge traditional patriarchy, Sidhwa does manage to weave a profound and ultimately optimistic narrative that offers many inspirations concerning the unbeatable, exhaustible female energy and strength to the readers all around the world. That's also why she is considered by many to be a pioneering figure of feminism from Pakistan. If she does not deserve the title, probably no one else does.

Chapter 15 Materialism and Its Psychological Burden: Reading Catherine Lim's "The Marriage" (Singapore)

"Catherine Lim's greatest strength seems to be her unusual ability to stand apart as an observer of Chinese behaviour patterns in Singapore."

——Ilsa Sharp, *Business Times*

"Catherine Lim does Singapore fiction proud with her simple, down-to-earth stories of the common life of common people written with such sharpness of observation and sensitivity as to render sublimity to what would otherwise be mundane affairs."

——Kee Thuan Chye, *The National Echo*

As one of the most outstanding and most daring voices in Singapore, Catherine Lim (1942–) never ceases to surprise, shock, delight, and instruct her numerous readers both at home and abroad with her fiction which gives a vivid and larger-than-life account of the many facets of contemporary Singapore society, especially the traditional Chinese culture and its impact on Singaporean women. So far, she has been awarded the prestigious Montblanc-NUS Centre for the Arts Literary Award and the S. E. A. Write Award, and made a Knight of the Order of Arts and Letters (France) and an ambassador of the Hans Christian Andersen Foundation (Copenhagen).

Written with wit and deliberate irony, *Little Ironies*, Lim's first collection of short stories and the first ever of its kind in her native country, may best be described as a collection of vignettes concerning modern Singapore life, mostly involving the Singaporean Chinese community. In each of the stories there is an ironic twist which recreates the stark and realistic modern life of the 1970s, informed by superstition, ignorance, snobbery and materialism. Among them, "The Marriage" bears great testimony to the subtle infiltration of the overwhelming global materialism into the psyches of not a few contemporary Singaporean men and women in their domestic life, as well as its unsettlingly destabilising effect.

Wealth and Status as Signifiers of Both Omnipotence and Nothingness

For not a few contemporary Singaporeans, the traditional Chinese notion of marriage as a business transaction and the alliance of powerful families is not challenged, but reinforced by the overwhelming global (largely western) materialism. When it comes to marriage, what is most valued in a man is often not his inherent goodness or true affection for the woman. Instead, such trappings as wealth and status become the most eloquent definers of what he is. However, since they are mere trappings, they cannot replace or substitute for true affection in a prolonged period. When the resurfacing true emotional needs are quenched after the end of fragile, short-lived material gratification, the hidden problems, anxieties and pains inevitably arise, often in an alarming way.

Helen, the young and beautiful heroine in "The Marriage", is such a Singaporean woman whose love life is unwittingly swayed by a host of forces that include everything but her own emotional needs and feelings. From the very beginning, she chooses, or rather is chosen by Ling Aw Siak, the super-rich, super-influential man in her country. On the surface, he has everything any social climbing woman envies: his dignified looks, his impeccably-tailored suit, his meticulously done hair, his wisdom-exhibiting eyes, his glamorous office and fancy car, combine to show the world that this is a man of men.

However, after the marriage, the simulacrum of its perfection soon crumbles down. Such a man of men turns out to be far from being perfect. First and foremost, he is old enough to be Helen's grandfather. All he needs is someone to fondle and play with, as well as to give him some "face" that becomes his status in public. It is by no means easy to bridge the generation gap. It is even harder for them to meet each other's physical and emotional needs. When the short-lived glamour in public is over, what is left in private is nothing but nothingness that comes with merely functional, often poorly-consummated sex deprived of love.

Apart from his old age, Ling Aw Siak's morbid inclination to show non-proportional suspicions even concerning the most minimal gesture or act on her part also troubles Helen. Every time some guy talks to her (either with the intention to seduce her or not), her excessively jealous husband is apt to put blame on her as if she were the seductive siren. Despite her great reluctance, she has to force herself to constantly placate him (instead of telling him to apologise), not because she loves him, but because she feels that she is obliged to do so— "The heavy-lidded eyes had looked at her slyly for a moment. 'One million. I gave you one million and your parents three hundred thousand on our marriage,' they seemed to say"① (59). Another reason for her placation of her husband is that she cannot allow her hard-won marriage to fail, in case of which she will be mercilessly ridiculed by her own parents, her husband's sons and daughters, as well as the scandal-seeking newspapers. Therefore, she can do nothing but see her sad marriage life drag on endlessly and hopelessly.

As can be seen above, in the social climbing heroine's life, wealth and status undergo a tremendous and unsettling change in their signifying processes. Initially, they seem to empower her in unprecedented ways in public. Later, however, they become vicious forces that subtly and yet unmistakably coerce her into silent and painful submission. Eventually, they even turn into signifiers of profound nothingness. Neither can they provide psychological security nor emotional comfort, rendering the heroine trapped and immured within her own home.

Transgressive Fantasies as Signifiers of Both Escape and Re-entrapment

For the emotionally impoverished wives in Singapore and elsewhere, the transgressive imagination or act often becomes a means to relieve themselves of the psychological burdens imposed by patriarchy and their own unwitting complicity. However, such escapist gestures often cost them greatly, for they often end up by reproducing the tragic

---

① Catherine Lim, *Little Ironies: Stories of Singapore* (Singapore: Heinemann Educational Books, 1978).

heroine's entrapment plot once again.

This is exactly the case with Helen, who secretly attempts to find ways out of her predicament in her husband's house. Kwang, a young man she accidentally meets at a social gathering, becomes such a potential site of her infinite fantasies for extramarital affairs. During that party, she already feels his secret and yet unmistakable gaze on her, which is deliberately avoided by her and yet secretly enjoyed. Later, when his letters that explicitly show his affection for her arrive, such fantasies become something solid, something that IS, even if she cannot allow herself to take liberties with herself in reality.

Such a self-deceptive liberation soon turns out to be a new form of entrapment. Helen knows that she cannot reciprocate her affection (no matter if it is love or merely emotional need) to Kwang. Yet, she secretly hopes that he will never stop showing his affections to her even in the absence of her direct and explicit encouragement. For Kwang, expectations of such a kind certainly go beyond his endurance and self-styled dignity. That's why Helen feels so dis-eased when she discovers Kwang time and again taking his girlfriend to places easily within her sight, as if he is deliberately having his revenge on her for her failure to reply. At a dinner party at the Dynast, he even proudly parades his girlfriend, now his fiancée, in front of her. Although she deliberately tries all means to feign indifference to Kwang's revengeful designs, she still cannot help being troubled time and again by this "betrayal". However, to her sadness, she indeed has no reason to blame anyone except herself.

As can be seen above, for the besieged wife, sexual fantasies both offer relief and produce new anxieties. Initially, they are contingently reassuring due to the new chances that they seem to be capable of providing for the woman. Ultimately, however, they are profoundly destabilising, for they are no less oppressive, challenging, and demanding than a marital relationship. Instead of getting rid of old anxieties, the wife has to grapple with new anxieties, which only pile themselves upon the old ones, threatening to drive her on the brink of insanity.

For Catherine Lim, modern experiences in today's world are so complicated that a mere glimpse of a fleeting moment in a domestic scene only hides many more untold stories waiting to be explored. Just as she herself comments on *Little Ironies*, "An accumulation, over the years, of small experiences, random observations and casual reflections which I thought I had forgotten, would persist in coming back and working itself first to the memo pads and then to the typewriter. The result is 'Little Ironies'." This simple description of her writing process only reminds us of the author's masterful, unique ability to capture small, seemingly trivial moments and shape them into immortal art.

Chapter 16 Unexpected Female Affinities and Reconciliations in a Riot in Chimamanda Ngozi Adichie's "A Private Experience" (Nigeria)

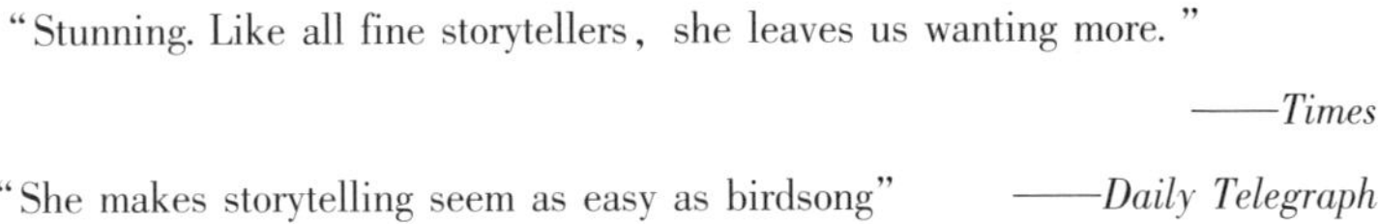

"Stunning. Like all fine storytellers, she leaves us wanting more."

——*Times*

"She makes storytelling seem as easy as birdsong" ——*Daily Telegraph*

Among all Nigerian women novelists working in English today, Orange-Prize winning author Chimamanda Ngozi Adichie (1977 –) never ceases to seduce readers with her well-crafted language, her creative story-telling, and profound human themes touching upon war, racial and ethnic conflicts, and their impact on ordinary lives.

In "A Private Experience", Adichie chooses a most unlikely setting to foreground the two main protagonists in the story: a deserted store in a riot. One by one, two women climb into the window of the store to escape being hurt or looted by runway rioters. Ironically, these two women are different in every possible way. Chika is Igbo and Christian, and obviously highly educated, while the woman (the narrator refrains from telling her name) is a Northerner with a strong Hausa accent, barely literate, and Muslim. Considering the long-time conflicts between these two racial and religious groups, they are initially quite alert to each other.

However, this alertness gradually loses its grip on these two women ironically linked together. In fact, from the very beginning of the story, Chika is somewhat led by this Muslim woman to this store for escape. Therefore, in her consciousness, she already feels that this woman may be not as violent in nature as Igbo Christians often accuse Muslims.

The following exchanges between these two women indeed prove the groundlessness of the fear they may harbour towards each other. Obviously, the woman is against the violence committed by Muslims in this riot, saying it is "a work of evil"[①] (50). After all, innocent Christian people are killed, and Muslim civilians' markets are also damaged. She never lets her faith blind her eyes to reality. On the other hand, Chika also gives the pregnant woman good advice on moisturizing the nipples so as to prevent them from being damaged. To forge a bond between them, she even invents a story of her mother also having begotten five children, just like this woman.

A further understanding comes when they both pray for the safety of each other's family members. This Muslim woman solemnly prays to Allah to keep Chika's sister and Halima in safe places. Chika also prays to God to keep the woman's daughter safe and sound, free from the harm brought about by this unexpected riot. This solemn, even ritualistic moment is highly moving, for it removes the highly limiting and inhuman boundaries set up by various parties or individuals, at least temporarily. God and Allah are both respected and invoked. Those

---

① Chimamanda Ngozi Adichie, *The Thing Around your Neck* (London: Fourth Estate, 2009). Subsequent citations to this work are given as parenthetical page references in the text.

who believe in either of them are understood, appreciated and respected. Both Chika and the woman have their "private experience" (52).

When she feels the danger is over, Chika insists on climbing out of the window, promising to be back to fetch the woman out. On the way back home, she chances upon many bodies that lie on the ground. Some of them are burnt so seriously that she can never tell if they are Muslims or Christians. This serves as a timely and silent comment that all men are the same in death. To fight in life for such useless purposes is indeed foolish.

When she does honour her promise to take the Muslim woman out, that woman is shocked to find blood on Chika's leg. She takes pains to dress her wound with the containers she finds in the store. Even in their departing moment, she still thinks of Chika's interests. This further impresses Chika so much that she finally knows the gentleness is indeed not the sole property of Ingo Christians. A Hausa and Muslim can bring equal warmness and gentleness. Before their departure, Chika asks the Muslim woman her scarf as a gift, a memory for what they have both been through. They both say to each other: "greet your people" (56). It should be noticed that "people" instead of "family" is used in the context, implying the hope for reconciliation not simply between individuals or small units, but between peoples.

Concerning this incident, BBC radio reports as such: "religious with undertones of ethnic tension" (55). For Chika, the enlightened one, such reporting no longer convinces her, for everything is "packaged and sanitized and made to fit into so few words" (55), hardly covering half of the truth here. The matter is far from being so simple, the people cannot be reduced to a single belongingness. Behind the capitalized "History" of violence, intolerance and hatred, there are also many other kinds of "histories" or "her-stories", such as one between her and the Muslim woman in their accidental encounter, which try not to be involved into this all-submerging "History", keep the best of human nature intact, and communicate and help each other in the most difficult and trying times. In fact, the BBC's partial reports infuriate Chika so much that she even wants to throw the radio outside.

The newspaper *The Guardian* also makes a reductive reading of this incident by saying "the revolutionary Hausa-speaking Muslims in the North have a history of violence against non-Muslims" (55). This high-sounding claim also becomes groundless in Chika's eyes, for in her private experience, she does feel "the gentleness of a woman who is Hausa and Muslim" (55). After all, to believe or not to believe, personal experience is the most eloquent standard. This is the most important and most humane message Adichie seeks to convey in this short story.

Chapter 17 Interrogating the "Either/or" Ideology on the Traumatic Body in Yvonne Vera's *Without a Name* (Zimbabwe)

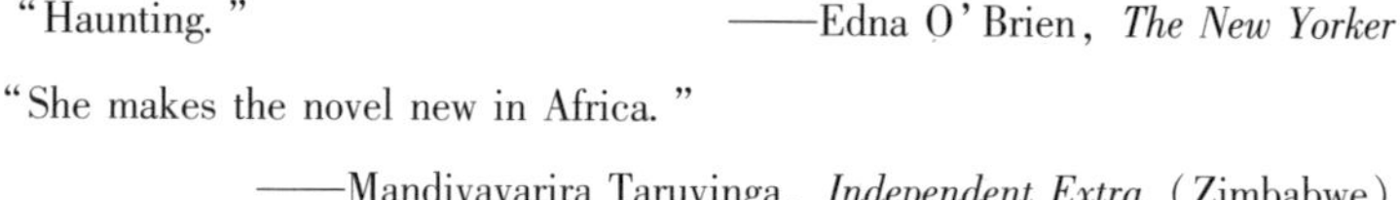

"Haunting." ——Edna O'Brien, *The New Yorker*

"She makes the novel new in Africa."

——Mandivavarira Taruvinga, *Independent Extra* (Zimbabwe)

In more than one sense, award-winning Zimbabwean novelist Yvonne Vera (1964 – 2005) emerges as a very striking presence in African women's literary world. The highly poetic language and largely violent, subversive themes that often dare to touch upon various taboos indeed reveal much of the unpleasant and grim reality in this war-torn country.

In *Without a Name*, Vera foregrounds a markedly sensitive time—1977, a time when the liberation war was raging in its most fierce manner. Colonists still desperately tried to retain their last stronghold, as well as their ideological and cultural influences. At the same time, nationalistic guerrilla also claimed equal, undivided loyalty and obedience from the Zimbabweans.

In the context of this "either/or" binary oppositions, Vera poses a very serious and unsettling question by portraying a victimised woman figure named Mazvita. For her, the master narratives by any outside forces seem to be equally oppressive and abusive, to the exclusion of women like her.

Specifically speaking, faced with the colonists, she certainly harbours strong hatred for their dispossession of her homeland, forcing her to go on endless exiles from place to place. However, the nationalistic guerrilla treats her no better. Not only do they reproduce the same hegemonic pattern and apply it to those citizens liberated by them, some of them even perpetrate severe bodily harms on them. In fact, Mazvita herself is violently raped by none other than a liberation soldier who even calls her "sister"① (35).

The rape of Mazvita is highly symbolic and much more. Certainly, it is a strikingly present sign of victimisation imposed by power itself on the powerless, no matter where it comes from (foreign invaders, domestic nationalists, etc). Or, as Grace Musila aptly argues, "(t)hrough Mazvita's rape..., Vera retrieves these banished narratives of ordinary people's less-glorifying experience of these heroic struggles and calls for the acknowledgment of the individual scars inflicted on individual lives"②. On a more profound and possibly ironic level, this raping incident is also a perverted awakening of Mazvita's awareness of individuality and the ensuing quest for self-discovery (or recovery). She starts to feel confused, doubting the assigned role and meaning of her existence. She feels herself to be without a name; her child is equally nameless.

This doubt is heightened during her respective stays with her lov-

---

① Yvonne Vera, (New York: Farrar, Straus and Giroux, 2002). Subsequent citations to this work are given as parenthetical page references in the text.

② Grace Musila, "Embodying Experience and Agency in Yvonne Vera's *Without a Name* and *Butterfly Burning*," *Research in African Literatures*, 38, no. 2 (2007), 54.

ers, namely Nyenyedzi and Joel. Despite the former's sympathy for her tragic past, he still feels that Mazvita needs disciplining before being a good woman, for she falls short of having a sufficient sense of the meaning of the homeland. In other words, she does not love her country and land enough. This version of archetypal or compulsory nationalism repulses Mazvita, especially concerning the fact that she herself is severely hurt and damaged by a nationalistic soldier. She really finds it more and more difficult to differentiate the colonists and the anti-colonial fighters in their basic nature and sinister intentions behind their respective acts. This fundamental departure in view finally destroys their relationship, setting Mazvita on the journey to the city Harare.

In Harare, Mazvita encounters her second lover Joel. They begin to lead a very strange life. No one tells or needs to tell each other anything about their past. They simply "live" together. For them, this amounts to following the rule of absolute freedom. However, this feigned and deliberately fashioned freedom is quickly shattered by Joel's knowledge of Mazvita's pregnancy. For him, this child is not wanted, for he is not his biological child. Despite Mazvita's sincere confessions, Joel fails to show any sympathy for this victimised lover, relentlessly driving her away onto another exile.

Twice abandoned, Mazvita cannot help feeling much aware of one truth—the concurrence and fundamental homogeneousness of oppressive hegemony and power in all forms, as well as their cruel and inhuman marginalisation of the minority groups or individuals. Colonialism, nationalism, male chauvinism—all these three dispossess one of his endowed rights and interests, and demand absolute, unconditional obedience. Among the powerless, women are certainly already fixed in the lowest rung, being forced to keep an eternally silent, absent presence, excluded from the grand master narratives.

This terribly bleak and yet ultimately true view of life leads Mazvita to commit an unthinkable act for desperate release of her long repressed emotions, or a desperate "response to, or rather revolt, against"① her traumatic experience—infanticide. This act renders her almost out of her mind—she keeps on saying that she has "broken the neck of her child" (109).

In a sense, this appalling occurrence of child-killing is attributed not only to Mazvita's equally narrow perspective on her life and future (she wants to change the nameless fate of her child and herself with this act), but also to the collective oppressive forces at work.

The redemption finally comes only when Mazvita returns to the place of her beginning—Mubaira where she is lovingly called her name "Mazvita" by her mother, remembers the various voices from this place, and intends to carry them on. Only then she "bends forward and releases the baby from her back, into her arms" (116). From "back" to "arms", the baby undergoes its ritual of symbolical transformation from an oppressive burden of trauma to a loving rebirth of hope for the future.

---

① Ruth Lavelle, "Yvonne Vera's *Without a Name*: Reclaiming That Which Has Been Taken," in *Sign and Taboo: Perspectives on the Poetic Fiction of Yvonne Vera*, ed. Robert Muponde and Mandi Taruvinga (Harare: Weaver Press, 2002), 110.

Chapter 18 Different Cast, Same Script: Reading Ama Ata Aidoo's "Two Sisters" (Ghana)

"Aidoo has reaffirmed my faith in the power of the written word to reach, teach, to empower and encourage." ——Alice Walker

"She writes from the heart." ——Hilda Twongyeiwe

As one of the most prominent literary voices in contemporary Ghana, Commonwealth Writers Prize (Africa Division) -winning Ama Ata Aidoo (1942–) is equally versed in writing dramas and fiction. Arguably, she is highly perceptive in detecting various post-colonial social ills that directly or subtly distort human minds, often in a rather ironic tone. As a woman, she pays particular attention to those drastic changes in ways of thinking and behavioural modes that unmistakably influence a whole range of contemporary Ghanaian women. In "Two Sisters", one of her most eloquent short stories, Aidoo carefully lays bare to the readers two sisters' markedly different reactions and responses to the whirlwind of social changes in Ghanaian political and daily life, as well as the ultimate entrapment into the abyssal world for both.

The First Option for Ghanaian Women: An Utilitarian Approach

For quite a few Ghanaian women who have got used to the ever-changing reality both domestically and internationally, the only useful thing that remains the same is the art of adaptability to any changes. For a better life, or mere survival, one (not to mention an underprivileged woman) has to be always highly alert to the changing political situation, practical and flexible in dealing with different people, especially those in the upper part of the social ladder. In other words, an utilitarian (not an ideal) approach becomes the first and the best (albeit quite disturbing to the readers) option for quite a few Ghanaian women.

This is exactly the case with Mercy, the younger sister in "Two Sisters". Ironically, the bearer of such a goddess-like name seems to be the very opposite of mercy. In a world still largely recovering from its colonial damages, she quickly learns to re-appropriate the colonial ideology (the eternal rule of power versus powerlessness) for her own practical use. Young, beautiful and ambitious, she desires the best of everything, and believes that she deserves everything. To be a mere typist (like most common people) for ever has never satisfied her. To achieve her ambitious goal, she can do anything, unhindered by any principle, ethical or religious. She can also be unhindered by any emotional concerns (she is hardly a woman prone to tears). Like a cool and highly experienced merchant, she knows her market value, and knows how to make full use of her body, charm and smartness. She also knows the wicked art of meticulous calculation, always choosing the very man who can bring her the largest profits in a relationship and cruelly abandoning any lesser candidate without fail. That's why she can secure the solid affection of Mensar-Authur (not the much younger and yet much less successful Joe), a prominent member of parliament before the coup, who does not hesitate to shower her with expensive handbags, beautiful new shoes and fancy cars that can provoke other girls' envy as she wishes.

The most shocking and yet highly truthful portrayal of Mercy's highly practical attitude and behavioral mode occurs when she eventually abandons the powerless Mensar-Authur at a lightening speed after the coop. Not only so, she quickly becomes the new mistress of Captain Ashley, one of the most prominent and visible members of the new ruling class in the post-coup era.

As can be seen, Mercy's greed for advantages and affiliation with powers profoundly and truly reflect the extent to which some Ghanaian women's minds are greatly distorted. To survive in a politically fragile situation, they become willing accomplices, sometimes even savage, sly and inhuman she-wolves. As long as they themselves can live, other people's lives are inconsequential. As long as they can get extra advantages, anyone can be their partner in a sex trade. This may sound terrible or exaggerating, but it is almost the logical conclusion reached by such women who follow their own line of thinking.

The Second Option for Ghanaian Women: A Conservative Approach

If the first option sounds too crass or too cruel, the second option, namely a conservative approach for Ghanaian women is no better. For these women, life (no matter how poor, unfavorable or terrible) is still livable and worth living. The constant changes cannot and should not change their own human nature, or their status as good and moral women. They should still cherish the old, traditional beliefs, values, and ways of life with steadfastness and sincerity. Otherwise, they are bound to lose their identity and identification. However, in a constant fight or conflict between their old beliefs and the new ones, even the most tradition-cherishing women are subjected to doubts, questionings and confusions.

This struggle is typified in Connie, the elder sister in "Two Sisters". Apparently, she is docile, non-ambitious, content with whatever life offers to her. She can hardly understand her younger sister's great impatience with her own life, or her unmentionable affairs with one after another man. She also fails to follow the logic of her own husband James' argument that everything Mercy has done is absolute right, thus deserving their admiration and encouragement; that they should use the social-climbing Mercy to get something (such as a car from abroad) for themselves.

Apart from the emotional turmoil caused by Mercy's inappropriate behaviours, her own husband's infidelity and abuse of her further throw Connie into existential doubts. Very much unlike her younger sister, Connie always remains faithful to James. However, her husband never repays her with his own faithfulness. Instead, he often goes out to find other women for sex, especially when she cannot perform her wifely duty during her pregnancy. For him, Connie is more like a child-bearing machine, forced to bear one child after another for him. She hates to be treated this way. However, she has no courage to question her husband in any way, not to mention the determination to divorce him.

As can be seen, Connie's conservative attitude towards everything and everyone around her also leads her nowhere but to confusion. This profoundly shows the severe problems with the other extreme of femininity: weakness, inertia, and lack of action.

In a society characterised by harshness, intolerance and endless changes, making a decision or choice (if there is really anything called "choice" in that context) for a woman is by no means easy. If one chooses to be Mercy, the Ghanaian Becky Sharp, one gains political favour at the cost of human dignity and morality; if one chooses to be Connie, the Ghanaian Amelia Sedley, one feels reassured for one's identification with tradition, though still hardly escaping the mental shock or confusion from the overwhelming immoral influences all around. If a Mercy can be a little bit more conscientious, or a Connie can be a little bit more courageous and daring (not necessarily aggressive), the post-colonial Ghana may be changed into a much better and more promising place, for both men and women.

Chapter 19 The Plight of Three Generations of Women in a Harsh World: Reading Lauri Kubuitsile's "The Rich People's School" (Botswana)

Among contemporary women writers living in Botswana, African Writers' Prize-shortlisted Lauri Kubuitsile is one that merits special mention, not least because she is extremely fruitful in that she practically writes anything. Among her various works, her short stories have garnered for her a very good reputation for its vivid and humanistic portrayal of Botswana life, especially that of Botswana women. For instance, in "The rich people's School", she manages to give voice to three generations of women who make all possible attempts to change the fate of themselves and their families. Despite the fact that not all attempts can yield fruit, their unyielding determination to struggle in a less friendly context is indeed profoundly moving and inspiring.

Mother: Desperately Seeking a New Life Elsewhere

Although the major character, Sylvia's mother, is largely absent in the text, she still makes her voice heard through Sylvia's truthful recollection. Like many women who refuse to be silently contained in a largely suffocating environment (a dry, backward desert and a place marked by polar extremes), Sylvia's mother desperately desires to change her fate. That's why she chooses to befriend an American and eventually marries him. Some critics tend to argue that her motive is quite suspicious, revealing her greed, materialism and blind worship of the west. However, it seems that they have overlooked the fact that it is by no means wrong to have the wish to improve oneself, to become better, to live better. Sylvia's mother simply wants to enjoy a life that can promise freedom and decency. When such an opportunity presents itself to her, her grasp of it is by no means a shameful act.

Not only does she try to change her own life, Sylvia's mother also wins our sympathy in that she tries very hard to change her daughter and her own mother's life as well. Although she cannot persuade her American boyfriend to take her daughter (dubbed by him as "Black Sylvia") and her own mother with her, she does try to provide for them in her own way. She never stops sending money back to her own mother, asking her to get Sylvia enrolled into the best possible school in Botswana. Some critics argue that money cannot replace a mother's companionship, care and love. However, they seem to have failed to take into consideration the specific context of this text. After all, every single penny sent from America is earned by the painstaking efforts of Sylvia's mother. Although she cannot be near her Botswana family, she has put all her care and love into the money sent to Sylvia, which should not be seen as a mere symbol of materialism. Her sacrifices should not be simply or easily dismissed.

Daughter: Trapped in a Discriminatory World

Different from her world-weary mother, Sylvia is by no means a sophisticated child. In fact, she is highly appreciative of her house, her surroundings, the weather, as well as the nature. She is also in full anticipation of her days at school.

However, even she cannot be immune from the negative impact from her highly discriminatory world that is full of binary oppositions in various kinds. For instance, when she is at the rich people's school (not the government school), she finds she has become the inevitable "other" in the eyes of practically everybody else there. For the white English-speaking woman who sits at the registration desk, she is simply unwelcome. The way she receives her large fees for schooling and writes out a paper is very nonchalant and indifferent. For the children there who are used to privileges and wealth, Sylvia is obviously not their type or kind. Even if she has the luck to be here, her money is still seen by them as suspicious, hiding her REAL social status. When they chance upon the humble food she brings there, they cannot help making fun of her and refuse to leave her alone. A boy even grabs her tumbler away from her, only to drop it on the ground and stamp hard on it with a vicious smile and even more vicious words to the effect that she should go away.

All these incidents make Sylvia feel ill at ease. She does not like to be reminded again and again of her poor origin. Nor does she like to study in a hostile world where practically everybody else treats her as the alien, the strange, the unwelcome. That' why she decides not to go to that rich people's school any more without telling her grandmother. However, she still asks her grandmother to drop her at the end of the road every morning and pick her up every afternoon at the same place. This is indeed deceptive, but with good intentions. Although still a child, little Sylvia does not want her grandmother to worry too much about her. Fortunately, even when her grandmother accidentally knows her white lie, Sylvia still wins her grandmother's understanding and sympathy, for they both know too well what it means to be in a place that is so much like another country.

Grandmother: Seeking a Practical and Sustainable Life in Her Homeland

Compared to Sylvia, still a child who has just been forced to know her place in the world, and her world-weary mother who desperately struggles with her own fate at all costs, Sylvia's grandmother has experienced more ups and downs in life, though with a steady sense of rootedness. She does not like her daughter to go elsewhere, even if it is the much-hyped America. However, she still chooses to respect her daughter's choice and keeps guard over her granddaughter without any complaints.

Of course, for a frail and resource-less old woman like her, this grandmother also has her own deeply-trenched fear and anger when she has to take her granddaughter to the equally much-hyped rich people's school. The facilities, the children from rich families, the registration staff, or practically everything and everyone there greatly unnerve her. However, she still insists on taking her granddaughter there, for she sincerely hopes that all hopes of changing their life reside in the education she will receive there. In her imagination, when Sylvia graduates from a good school like this, she may enter a good university and later become someone influential, such as a lawyer or a doctor, unlike her daughter who she believes has sold her life away.

It has to be noted that when she eventually discovers Sylvia's school-missing behaviour, she does not blame her right away. Instead, she asks her kindly why she does so. After hearing the explanations made by Sylvia, she does show her understanding, for she truly feels the pressures felt by her granddaughter, who is equally weak and yet equally persistent in trying to cope with the harsh reality. That's why she decides to get her granddaughter enrolled in another school near their house. In that way, she can achieve both goals: on the one hand, her granddaughter does not have to suffer from any humiliations from those rich people's children and grow normally and happily. On the other hand, she can save some money for her daughter in the United States, who can use it to travel back to them. For her, a family get-together in her homeland is something she truly and most values.

Arguably, the choices made by these three generations of women in a country still characterised by binary oppositions and discrimination seem to be quite different. Yet, what they all share in common is a rare willpower to come to terms with their plight and the persistence in seeking various ways and strategies so that they and their family members can lead a more decent and more promising life in the future. In other words, there is no single best choice, there is no one standard to judge what they do and think. As long as they have tried their best and remain deeply optimistic before the many pitfalls ahead, they have already made a big difference. That's also why this story of Lauri Kubuitsile's can still move readers so much.

Works Cited

[1] SHUSHA GUPPY. Interview: the art of fiction XCVII: Anita Brookner [J]. Paris Review, 1987 (109): 150.

[2] ANITA BROOKNER. Falling slowly [M]. New York: Vintage Books, 2000.

[3] CHERYL ALEXANDER MALCOLM. Understanding Anita Brookner [M]. Columbia, South Carolina: University of South Carolina, 2002.

[4] WAYNE C BOOTH. The rhetoric of fiction [M]. Chicago: University of Chicago Press, 1983.

[5] CLAIRE KEEGAN. Antarctica [M]. New York: Grove Press, 1999.

[6] ALEKSANDAR HEMON. Best European fiction 2011 [M]. Champaign and London: Dalkey Archive Press, 2010.

[7] MAUREEN RYAN. Marilynne Robinson's *Housekeeping*: the subversive narrative and the new American Eve [J]. South Atlantic Review, 1991, 56 (1): 86.

[8] MARIA MOSS. The search for sanctuary: Marilynne Robinson's *Housekeeping* and E. Annie Proulx's *The Shipping News* [J]. Amerikastudien/American Studies, 2004, 49 (1): 83.

[9] MAGGIE GALEHOUSE. Their own private Idaho: transience in Marilynne Robinson's *Housekeeping* [J]. Contemporary Literature, 2008, 41 (1): 118.

[10] ALICE MUNRO. Friend of my youth [M]. New York: Vintage Books, 1991.

[11] EMILY LISTFIELD. Straight from the heart [J]. Harper's Bazaar, 1990, 123: 82.

[12] JAMAICA KINCAID. Annie John [M]. London: Vintage Books, 1997.

[13] J BROOKS BOUSON. Jamaica Kincaid: writing memory, writing back to the mother [M]. Albany: State University of New York Press, 2005.

[14] MOIRA FERGUSON. Jamaica Kincaid: where the land meets the body [M]. Charlottesville and London: University Press of Virginia, 1994.

[15] LEIGH GILMORE. The limits of autobiography: trauma and testimony [M]. Ithaca: Cornell University Press, 2001.

[16] SUE KOSSEW. Lighting dark places: essays on Kate Grenville [M]. Amsterdam: Rodopi, 2010.

[17] KATE GRENVILLE. Lilian's story [M]. Edinburgh: Canongate, 2007.

[18] JANET FRAME. The daylight and the dust: selected short stories [M]. London: Virago Press, 2010.

[19] JACINTA GALEA I. A novel in prose and poetry [D]. Hawaii: University of Hawaii, 2005.

[20] SIA FIGIEL. Where we once belonged [M]. New York: Kaya Press, 1999.

[21] YIYUN LI. Gold boy, emerald girl [M]. New York: Random House, 2010.

[22] MALLIKA A NAIR. "A Room of One's Own": the metaphori-

cal implications of "House" in Shashi Deshpande's novels [J]. Indian Literature, 2010, 54 (4): 178.

[23] CATHERINE LIM. Little ironies: stories of Singapore [M]. Singapore: Heinemann Educational Books, 1978.

[24] CHIMAMANDA NGOZI ADICHIE. The thing around your neck [M]. London: Fourth Estate, 2009.

[25] YVONNE VERA. *Without a name* and *Under the tongue* [M]. New York: Farrar, Straus and Giroux, 2002.

[26] GRACE MUSILA. Embodying experience and agency in Yvonne Vera's *Without a name* and *Butterfly burning* [J]. Research in African Literatures, 2007, 38 (2): 54.

[27] ROBERT MUPONDE, MANDI TARUVINGA. Sign and taboo: perspectives on the poetic fiction of Yvonne Vera [M]. Harare: Weaver Press, 2002.

Afterword

It is indeed with both relief and trepidation that I finally finish the last sentence in this book. The relief is, after one year's painstaking efforts, this book finally assumes its present form; the trepidation is, nothing is perfect, my book included.

The idea to write a book on contemporary women's writing first occurred as early as September 2011, when I just started my career as a college teacher in School of Foreign Languages, China University of Political Science and Law. At that time, despite the diversity of courses available to students, those related to literature, especially women's literature, were far and few between. As a scholar who is more than interested in women's writing (especially contemporary English-language fiction by women), I managed to open a course titled "A Survey of British and American Feminist Fiction", with very good reception among students, many of whom strongly believed that despite the fact that I was a man, I could perceive and understand women's plight and sufferings even better than women, and they were more than eager to hear more of my views on the woman question today. That's certainly one of the most important reasons why I have been able to stick to such an area of research since then. I am truly grateful to my students who have strengthened my belief in myself for all these years.

During the writing of the book, many colleagues and friends of mine also provide timely help to me. Thanks go to Professor Li Li,

Dean of School of Foreign Languages, who never fails to give me due recognition and encouragement in my most dire moments; Professor Sha Lijin, Vice Dean of School of Foreign Languages, who has told me time and again to persist in my pursuit of literary criticism despite the overwhelming influence from the legal discipline in my context; Associate Professor Shi Hongli, who has offered so many consolatory words to me during the most difficult time of my writing; Dr. Li Danling, who has kindly helped proofread some chapters of the book. And Professor Zhao Xiufeng, Professor Ma Hailing, my graduate students Lei Min and Yang Wei...It is practically impossible to complete the list!

It is known to all that pursuing a path of literary criticism in China is by no means lucrative. However, for me, it is indeed full of riches with which nothing else can compete. With so many good people faithfully around me, I never feel lonely. It is my sincere hope that this book can help you better understand and appreciate literature, especially contemporary women's fiction.

ZHANG Lei

July 2015, Beijing